It had been ten v...
Lucian Monrayne...
moment to perfection.

Every royal—major and minor—on the continent was present. Every prime minister. Every president. The crème de la crème of societies both modern and traditional mingled today to witness a spectacle Lucian personally found repulsive. But best of all were the cameras. There were *so* many cameras covering every possible angle, which was exactly what he needed.

He'd visualized this moment over and over, yet for all the mental preparation, he hadn't factored in the impact the cathedral itself would have on him—the deep ache of familiarity, the slicing regret as he took each step farther inside. He couldn't allow such distraction or self-indulgence. This moment was vital and he needed to be alert. Yet being here was like taking a spear to the heart—striking deep and releasing something he'd long suppressed. After an eternity adrift, he was *home*. And it almost unraveled him.

So he stared at her instead. The woman. He'd stopped the second Zara had turned. Not what he'd intended but he suddenly couldn't take another step.

Natalie Anderson

BACK TO CLAIM HIS CROWN

HARLEQUIN
PRESENTS

HARLEQUIN®
PRESENTS™

Recycling programs
for this product may
not exist in your area.

ISBN-13: 978-1-335-59280-4

Back to Claim His Crown

Copyright © 2023 by Natalie Anderson

For questions and comments about the quality of this book,
please contact us at CustomerService@Harlequin.com.

Harlequin Enterprises ULC
22 Adelaide St. West, 41st Floor
Toronto, Ontario M5H 4E3, Canada
www.Harlequin.com

Printed in U.S.A.

USA TODAY bestselling author **Natalie Anderson** writes emotional contemporary romance full of sparkling banter, sizzling heat and uplifting endings—perfect for readers who love to escape with empowered heroines and arrogant alphas who are too sexy for their own good. When she's not writing, you'll find Natalie wrangling her four children, three cats, two goldfish and one dog... and snuggled in a heap on the sofa with her husband at the end of the day. Follow her at natalie-anderson.com.

Books by Natalie Anderson

Harlequin Presents

The Night the King Claimed Her
The Boss's Stolen Bride

Billion-Dollar Christmas Confessions

Carrying Her Boss's Christmas Baby

Innocent Royal Runaways

Impossible Heir for the King

Jet-Set Billionaires

Revealing Her Nine-Month Secret

Rebels, Brothers, Billionaires

Stranded for One Scandalous Week
Nine Months to Claim Her

Visit the Author Profile page
at Harlequin.com for more titles.

For Kat—here's to 50 before 60—we got this!!!

CHAPTER ONE

'It needs several more stitches, Princess.'

Zara Durant gritted her teeth and remained dutifully still while the severe tailor secured her dress with surgical precision. She'd been standing for over two hours already but today everything needed to be perfect. If her bodice slipped and exposed her to a cathedral full of people, that would *not* be perfect—so it wasn't too hard to summon patience while multiple hair and make-up artists hovered, occasionally swooping close to enact other minor adjustments. She'd unintentionally lost a little weight in the run-up. Her mother had been delighted this morning when she'd finally arrived in Monrayne and seen Zara for the first time in weeks. The brusque seamstress not so much.

Monrayne was the smallest but wealthiest nation on the Scandinavian peninsula, famed for its pristine alpine environment, gleaming palaces and glittering modernity. Zara had been stunned when she'd driven through the city for the first time just over a week ago. It was a snow globe perfect scene with its tall spires, ancient architecture and sparkling snow-capped surroundings.

Right now, as the emergency alterations were made

to Zara's dress, her too-proud mother, the Queen of Dolrovia, was taking her seat in Monrayne's magnificent stone cathedral. Zara watched her mother's sweeping entrance on the television screen that had been set up in her suite. Millions were watching the live stream, including her invalid father, King Harold, in his bedroom back in Dolrovia. Their much smaller, much less wealthy country bordered the Baltic Sea and her father had been deposed just over a decade ago. The revolution had been peaceful but complete—their titles were now purely honorific and almost the only thing that remained of their history. The only property they'd been allowed to keep was the crumbling castle deep in the lowland plains. The other properties, plus the art, jewels and antiques, had moved to public ownership. But, despite rejecting their Royal family, her country—indeed the whole world—was fascinated by Zara's wedding today.

Clearly loving every moment, her mother imperiously acknowledged the hundreds of dignitaries, politicians, royals and celebrities who'd gathered in their finest couture to witness the Royal wedding of the decade—revelling in the resurgence of the kind of attention that had faded for their particular family a number of years ago.

Becoming powerless, penniless officially 'ex' Royals hadn't been easy for Zara's elderly parents, despite the fact the situation had been decades in the making. They believed it was because they lacked a male heir—nothing to do with their own denial of reality, their own continued excesses, their own failure to adapt to the modern world. They'd never imagined that their very late lamb—an unplanned, unnecessary, unwanted extra

girl who'd rarely been allowed past the castle gate—
would secure such an advantageous marriage contract.
That there was interest in their dusty lineage once more
was something they would make the most of.

So many citizens in Dolrovia were suddenly interested in the youngest princess, who hadn't been seen
in so long most had forgotten she even existed. She'd
been stuck there in the countryside, caring for disin-
terested parents, while her much older sisters lived in
the city. If Zara failed to show at the ceremony now
there wouldn't just be outrage but complete condemnation—and that was only from her parents.

It still didn't seem real, but the fact was *she* was
the bride in this spectacle. Furthermore, she'd not just
agreed to this madness, she'd actively pursued the position. She was marrying the Crown Prince of Monrayne—the head of a Royal family most definitely still
brimming with money, prestige and real power.

Not that *she* wanted these things. She wanted greater
personal freedom, and that was far more precious. And
it was that which she'd been promised. When born
to a life like hers, one had to seize opportunities and
strike bargains.

Now Zara stared at the stranger in the mirror. The
hours taken to create this fairy-tale facade had been
worth it. Her make-up was flawless. The diamond-encrusted hand-made lace covered her back and arms,
hiding the unsightly pink mottling that smothered her
skin when she was nervous. It also gave her a modest,
innocent air, one they apparently considered crucial.
She considered it archaic. But she gritted her teeth,
determined to forget the mortifying questioning from
the Crown Prince's advisors and the utterly humiliat-

ing examination she'd subsequently endured before being deemed an acceptable bride.

'I'm finished.' The seamstress spoke in English, the second language that both nations shared and that Zara spoke fluently.

Moments later, Zara slowly followed one of the liveried footmen, allowing the attendants a final hypercritical inspection as she passed. Despite their wafting air of disapproval, she was grateful for their frosty insistence upon perfection.

Monrayne's palace was far larger and more opulent than her castle on the verge of collapse and it was ridiculously easy to get lost in. The portraits which had once hung in the main atrium, but had since been sequestered in the furthest wing in which she'd been confined for this last week, had been way-finders for her. The first depicted the late Queen Kristyn and King Lucas on their wedding day. The second was of their only child, Prince Lucian. As always, Zara's glance lingered on the young man. His arresting gaze always caught her attention—those pale blue eyes, that winning smile, the heart-stopping handsomeness for ever young. The portrait had been painted when he was only sixteen—two years before his tragic disappearance in a diving accident a decade ago.

Zara had barely been thirteen but she remembered the global outpouring of grief and shock when it had happened. The frantic searches in the Mediterranean had gone on for weeks but his body had never been recovered. He'd been immensely popular, the dreamy Prince Charming of billions of girls all over the world. The elite boarding school he'd attended had been oversubscribed fifty times over as every wealthy family on the continent and beyond had tried to get their daughters alongside him in class. His mother, Queen Kristyn—already widowed—hadn't recovered from the loss and had died within days of the young man's death.

And now Zara was about to marry Lucian's cousin Anders, who'd become the new Crown Prince of Monrayne on Lucian's passing. He would be crowned King in just a few days when he came of Monraynian regal age on his twenty-fifth birthday. Their wedding today was merely the first of an elaborate series of celebrations, each bigger than the last.

The wedding. The birthday. The coronation.

She'd not been Prince Anders's first pick. His uncle, Garth—currently Regent of Monrayne—had discreetly visited her parents' castle. Her sisters had dropped everything and made one of their rare visits home to welcome him 'properly'. His query had taken them by surprise. That he was quietly searching for a suitable bride for the Crown Prince had sounded like something from the last century. Mia, the eldest, had politely explained that she was already in a serious relationship, while Ana had also declined, noting that at thirty-three she felt too old for Anders.

That was when Zara had stepped from the corner to volunteer. She'd stunned everyone. But while she might be ten years younger than Ana, she was old enough to make up her own mind. She was capable of far more than either her parents or her siblings knew.

Garth—who'd unsurprisingly forgotten her existence, given her cloistered life—had assessed her with calculating eyes and, to everyone's astonishment, had immediately agreed.

He'd admitted later than he'd not realised she would be there. To the world she was still the late arrived child, the much younger sister of the two beautiful princesses who'd embraced Dolrovia's democratic revolution while their parents had been forced to retreat from public life and curb all excesses.

Of course, there'd been caveats before complete agreement of the marriage contract. There'd been requirements to complete, including that absolute awkwardness…but then there'd been acceptance and surprising speed. It was less than two months since that initial meeting.

The terms were simple. She couldn't overshadow her future husband—no problem, given she disliked publicity and didn't court self-promotion. She was more than happy to stand supportively in the background. Because in private there could be more freedom than she currently had. She would be able to support charitable causes close to her heart and she might actually earn some respect from her family—but an element of freedom from them at the same time. Because she wasn't precious to them, in fact the opposite. Expected to be dutiful while being ignored and ill-educated at the same time, this was the only acceptable escape from the castle-bound life they'd prescribed for her.

Yet as she entered the eight-horse-drawn crystal carriage that would now take her to the cathedral, doubt almost devastated her. She breathed deeply, telling herself her nerves were only because she was the focal point for millions of people. She wasn't used to the spotlight. But today would be the worst. It would only get easier. She would remain in the background after this moment because the King had primacy. She'd be the safe option Garth had said they wanted.

Ten minutes later the carriage stopped outside the cathedral. She swallowed back nausea. She felt very alone. But then she'd been alone almost all her life.

Neither of her sisters were her bridal attendants. Mia and Ana had left home when Zara had been young. They rarely visited and when they did it was only to emphasise Zara's 'duty' to her parents and how perfectly her life suited her. So when Garth had decided that a bridal party of delightful children would be the thing, Zara had readily agreed. She didn't mind that she didn't know the children nor got to choose anyone else. She had few personal friends. So now she carefully held the stunning bouquet, maintained the smile the stylists had made her practice for hours and followed the assortment of sweet-looking offspring of favoured courtiers in petite silk dresses and sailor suits. Everything looked perfect. Even her. It was quite the miracle.

Breathe. Walk. Slowly. Carefully. Evenly. Calmly.

It didn't matter that she barely knew Anders. This was a political arrangement, not personal. There was plenty of time to get to know him. Yes, she was a little forlorn that he'd been too busy to see her this week. That there'd been no time for the two of them to be alone *at all* in their engagement. The many photos of them spread across the Internet had been the result of a single day's shoot which had involved another massive array of make-up artists and stylists.

He didn't turn to watch her walk towards him now. It was probably protocol. She ought to know, but she'd been so nervous at the rehearsals she hadn't really heard the detailed explanations why all these things were done in such convoluted ways. Yet, despite their fondness for tradition, the courtiers had been unashamedly delighted that she had no escort to walk her up the aisle as her elderly father was too infirm. Apparently, it would give everyone an unrestricted view of her elaborate dress. Diamond-studded, it was a gleaming work of art and masked the fact that Zara was no true beauty but merely a smaller, less vivid rendering of her stunning elder sisters.

She counted through the music and took each careful slow step over the centuries-old stones beneath her feet. But just as she finally passed the halfway mark she heard another sound repeating behind her. It took a moment to realise it was other footsteps on the flagstones. Heavier ones, moving a touch faster than her own—catching up to her, in fact. She faltered. The bride was supposed to be the last to arrive. Should she pause and allow whoever it was to get themselves seated?

As she hesitated the organ stopped. Then the trumpets. She hadn't actually made it all the way up the aisle, yet now the cathedral was abruptly silent.

Except for those heavy footsteps. They kept going.

She was a full ten feet short of where she was supposed to stop. But there didn't seem a lot of point to keep going when the music had stopped as well. She looked towards Garth, the chief architect of this entire pageant and her advisor in all of this. To her astonishment, as she watched he changed colour—first turning pale before his skin was suddenly awash with red. It was only deep emotion that caused an uncontrollable reaction like that.

Garth didn't meet her enquiring gaze but stared hard

behind her, his expression aghast. Anders, her groom, finally turned. He didn't so much as glance at her but also immediately fixated on the person coming up the aisle behind her. His jaw dropped but the rest of him stayed still, apparently transfixed.

She was being upstaged on her wedding day, even when wearing the world's most ludicrously expensive wedding dress with its diamond-encrusted lace. It was so typical that she couldn't get through this like a *proper* princess would. Not only was her title merely a superficial nod to placate her elderly parents, she didn't have the education or the experience, nor the looks nor even the polish she needed to really pull this off.

There were hundreds of people inside the cathedral. Hundreds of *thousands* lining the streets outside. Yet it was eerily silent except for those footsteps. She straightened her shoulders and made herself turn.

It was a man. A mountain of a man. Tall and unbelievably broad-shouldered, his muscular frame dominated her vision. He simply consumed the space of the aisle. As she turned, he stopped walking—now only three feet away—and stared right back at her.

He was clad in full ceremonial attire—*regal* attire. Black trousers...starched white jacket. The scarlet sash across his shoulder emphasised the menacing breadth of him. His hair was cropped close in military fashion, making his facial structure prominent—high cheekbones, square jaw and a nose that looked like it might have been broken more than once. He had an incongruously full mouth but it was currently tightly held, while a jagged, puckered scar cut through his left eyebrow and into his eyelid. She suspected he was lucky to still see from that eye. He was motionless now but he emanated repressed energy—*anger*.

Her heart frantically shoved burning blood through her body. She felt entirely alight—as if she'd somehow spontaneously combusted yet was still standing. He said nothing. He didn't seem to so much as breathe. But he stared back at her. The rest of the world blurred until she saw only him in the vast cathedral. It was as if they were utterly alone and then she felt the strangest compulsion to step towards him—to reach out, pulled by the emotion barely banked within him. She didn't. She was too lost in the palest, iciest eyes she'd ever seen.

In fact she'd seen eyes that colour only once before. In a portrait hanging in the corridor of the palace she'd just come from.

In a portrait of a dead man.

CHAPTER TWO

IT HAD BEEN ten very long years but Lucian Monrayne had picked his moment to perfection. Every Royal—major and minor—on the continent was present. Every prime minister. Every president. There were generals and dukes, authors and actors, models and musicians. The crème de la crème of societies both modern and traditional mingled today to witness a spectacle Lucian personally found repulsive. But best of all were the cameras. There were so *many* cameras covering every possible angle, which was exactly what he needed.

He'd visualised this moment over and over, yet for all the mental preparation he hadn't factored the impact the cathedral itself would have on him—the deep ache of familiarity, the slicing regret as he took each step further inside. The times he'd spent in here as a boy flashed in his head—memories he had no time or emotional capacity for now. He couldn't allow such self-indulgent distraction. This moment was vital and he needed to be alert. Yet being here was like taking a spear to the heart—it struck deep and released something long suppressed. After an eternity adrift he was *home*. And it almost unravelled him.

So he stared at her instead. The woman. He'd

stopped the second she'd turned. Not what he'd intended, but he suddenly couldn't take another step.

She was a few feet from him, a short figure in an enormous jewel-encrusted gown that had to be heavy for her slight frame to wear. Her white-blonde hair was swept back from her face, while the whole of her was enveloped in a gossamer veil. Beneath it he saw her elfin face—pointed chin, smooth skin, full rose-coloured lips and big eyes a far deeper blue than his own. Blue eyes that seemed to search right into him as if seeking out his soul.

She'd been the impetus in this. The cause of an opportunity he didn't think he'd have and that he couldn't ignore. If he had any humanity he would feel sorry for her. But his humanity had gone. All that remained was the survivor he'd been forced to become. A warrior. A strategist. He was a disciplined shell burnished by shame. So there was no soul for her to see.

But he would ruthlessly reclaim his rights, not because he deserved them, but because others deserved them even *less*. And yes, he would have some small revenge. He would finally do his duty. He would protect his kingdom and his people properly—give them the time he'd taken away. Guilt scoured him but determination steeled him.

And yet still in this most crucial of moments all he could do was stare at the woman in white. Time hung, the vision of her overwhelming him. She gleamed like a beacon of serenity, calming the chaos churning inside. He was instinctively drawn to her light—he who'd hid in the shadows for so very long.

The silence seemed endless. No one in the room

breathed. Not her. Not him. Not any of the hundreds around them. So the sound—when it finally came—roared.

'Lucian! Lucian! *Lucian!*'

His name crashed into the cathedral in waves, each increasingly louder and more passionate. They were the cries of the commoners beyond the palace walls. The ones watching the large screens that had been specially erected for today's extravaganza. The chant rapidly became deafening and reminded him why he was here. Because it was the name he'd not been called by in the same decade. He was the prince feared drowned long ago. Breathing. Returned at last.

Lucian finally forced his focus to the ruddy-faced fury standing to the right of her. Garth. Then to the rear of her. To the cruel. To the coward. His cousin and would-be assassin. Anders. Currently frozen in fury.

Lucian lifted his hand. There was the barest delay from the telecast but almost instantly the crowds outside hushed—attentive, agog.

'I suppose you didn't think you'd ever see me again, did you, cousin?' he muttered huskily, opting for English, the language common to most present.

He ignored the collective intake of breath of over a thousand people. He would have found it theatrically comical if he weren't so bitter. But bitter he was.

The last time he'd looked Anders in the eye was as he'd sunk beneath the water. He'd never forgotten the malevolent glint in his younger cousin's gaze and his almost gleeful intake of breath as the blood poured, blinding Lucian. He'd wanted to dismiss it as a nightmare—a figment of a confused, concussed brain, his memory filling the blanks with some warped version of events. But the vision was clear. He'd dived and hit his head—that *had* been an accident. But his young cousin had not attempted to rescue him. Anders had lifted the boat hook not to help Lucian out, but to strike another blow.

'You're an impostor.' Garth stepped forward.

Of course it was Garth who answered. Garth the puppet master. The one who'd wanted control from the start. Not Royal by blood, but whose nephew was. The man who'd been de facto ruling Monrayne, his corruption deepening through the decade. He'd siphoned riches for himself while trying to control—*hide*—the increasing cruelty of his nephew. Hence this distasteful charade today.

'Prince Lucian has been dead for a decade,' Garth added. 'Where have you been all this time—getting plastic surgery to try to pull off this elaborate ruse? It won't work.'

'I decided against plastic surgery,' Lucian said calmly. 'I have no desire to hide *any* of the wounds I've suffered.'

Gasps rippled through the cathedral. Anders looked greenish now. Wide-eyed, he remained half hiding behind his bride. Of course.

She hadn't moved either. That perfect princess still glittered in the light. The one he couldn't help looking at.

He'd endured that decade of banishment, waiting for this—the most public moment to reveal himself. To have his revenge on the man-child who'd tried to take everything from him and who'd succeeded in some ways Lucian still couldn't bear to acknowledge. He couldn't be distracted and fail now. So he welcomed the cold anger that rose in the wake of memories too hideous to allow. Anger was the best emotion of all.

'Allow me to show you.' Lucian steadily unbuttoned his jacket.

It hadn't been made by the tailors of Monrayne palace but those of King Niko of Piri-nu—no less valid, frankly more soft against his hardened skin. Finally unfastened, he let the jacket slide down his arms. With a soft swish it slipped to the floor. There was another collective intake of breath.

He'd deliberately worn nothing beneath it—a perfectly normal choice for the temperatures on the Pacific Island kingdom where he'd lived out this time, but here in Monrayne the cold bit. He refused to let it penetrate.

He also wore no bulletproof vest. In theory, someone could step up behind him and make an attempt, but his hearing was attuned. Plus he'd brought one guard with him, who was watching his six right now. If a sniper wanted to take him they'd go for a headshot anyway. But they wouldn't want blood spattered on the bride's beautiful dress. Not in front of an audience of millions. He'd counted on that.

So he stood in the centre of the cathedral. Bare-chested. His not-so-ceremonial sword at his side.

But, after all this time, it wasn't his enemy he watched. It was her. She still hadn't moved but her gaze dipped. He saw her curiosity. But something else bloomed as her gaze raked over the skin that he'd barely shown anyone, let alone the entire world all at once. For a flash he felt vulnerable. He was never this exposed. Her attention lingered on his tattoo. Then moved to the scar he'd had for most of his life. The scar the whole of Monrayne knew he had.

As her focus slowly slid even lower his entire body tensed. He was battered and scarred but he needed strength now and as he stared at her he felt it surging within him. All that should matter was *beyond* her. Yet he couldn't take his eyes off his ethereally beautiful bride. Her lashes lifted and for a second he thought he saw heat in her eyes. Surely not. Not a woman about to wed another man.

But then she nodded, almost imperceptibly, and it gave him the impetus he needed.

'You'll see the scar from the ice-skating accident I had when I was three.' He lifted his voice for all to hear—all anger and authority and using more words than he sometimes spoke in a day. 'And, as you can see, I've acquired a few more since.'

Everyone knew about the ice-skating accident. The permanent scar on his ribs had been documented in embarrassing paparazzi photos of him as a youth.

'Does anyone here desire to draw my blood *again*?' he asked coolly.

It was a direct, deliberate challenge. An unsubtle hint that the accident hadn't really been an *accident*. He'd become aware that there'd been rumours and speculation in the kingdom for years, and of course his body had never been found. But he *had* been declared dead and his cousin Anders pronounced heir. But Anders's guardian and uncle, Garth, had become the Regent, despite not being in the royal bloodline, because Monrayne liked its kings mature. Garth hadn't dared meddle with the ancient laws of succession. Besides which, it had suited him to retain power for as long as possible. But twenty-five was mere days away for Anders now.

'Naturally I will provide a sample for a DNA test. We will live stream that draw and put a tracker on the sample. We will keep the world's eyes on it while it is tested.' Lucian finally looked at Garth again. 'Won't we, Garth?'

There would be no mix-up or loss of his sample. Garth now understood this was no bluff and he didn't like it. He paled but inclined his head in mute agreement.

'I understand how much of a shock this is.' Lucian allowed his gaze to slide to the groom. 'Especially for my young cousin Anders.'

Anders hadn't moved a muscle. They were dressed in identical ceremonial attire. But Anders had no right to wear the sash of the Crown Prince. Not then. Not now. Not *ever*. He might be next in line to the throne but Lucian would do everything required to prevent that from happening.

It was the woman who broke the tableaux. He watched as she glided closer in that sparkling dress. Her gaze was locked on him and once more he found he couldn't tear his own away. It was wrong. Peripherals were important. The soldier within—mercenary really—knew prioritising her was foolish. But once more the world around them disappeared. She stopped a foot away. Her full focus on him this close was like an unbearably soft caress on his bare skin. And to his astonishment—and even more astonishing *pleasure*—she gracefully dropped into a deep curtsey.

'King Lucian.' She pitched her voice perfectly so the cathedral acoustics picked up her words. There wouldn't be a person present who wouldn't have heard her acknowledgement of his identity.

He didn't know her name. He should have, of course. He'd worked hard to restore his mental acuity and hadn't slipped in years. So this was vexing. He gritted his teeth and quickly covered the lapse.

'Princess.' He inclined his head.

He knew there were allies here. Those who did not wish to see Anders take the Crown. Those who knew something of the truth of the man. Lucian had done his research. But there were things he could learn only by being here on the ground and he had not expected Anders's bride to be the first to acknowledge him.

After a moment an army general left his position at the end of the second row and marched towards him. Lucian's intelligence had kept him apprised of the factions within the court and this older soldier had long been a servant of Monrayne. A sheen of emotion glistened in the older man's eyes. He didn't bow. He knelt in front of Lucian. His bones almost creaked with the effort.

'King Lucian,' he echoed huskily. 'Long live the King.'

Because Lucian was more than twenty-five. He was twenty-nine. Thus he was automatically King, whether he'd been officially crowned or not. He should've been the King for years already. But he'd been presumed dead. And he'd been hiding, biding his time for this rarest of opportunities.

Everyone in the cathedral was already standing but now his citizens bowed from the waist. The rulers of other nations nodded in acknowledgement at least.

'King Lucian.' The chant rang through the cathedral. 'Long live King Lucian!' Over and over and over again.

A swell of bitter rejection rose inside. He was not worthy to be King. But Anders was a worse alternative. So he would do what he had to do. He allowed it for a few moments, to let it fully sink in to Anders. To Garth. That he was back. And he let the anger resurge. Yet, even so, he couldn't take his gaze from the pretty woman, pale in that resplendent dress. Now the icy anger *burned*. Because anyone who knew Anders well—and Garth knew him—would know the man's tendencies and inclinations. And yet here was this ethereal, petite princess looking too perfect to even be real, about to be sacrificed to him. Did *she* know Anders—the truth of him? Or did she not care about those he'd hurt? Did she think herself safe somehow? Not even Lucian had been safe. That cold anger seeped out, driving him to test them both.

'Please don't let me interrupt the wedding a moment longer.' He bowed slightly towards the bride. 'I apologise for the hold-up in proceedings.'

The flicker of reproach in her gaze stabbed. He tensed, more alert than he'd been all week. The greatest threat to anyone present—to both this woman and to *himself*—was right now. But he was ready.

'*What?*' Anders finally stepped into Lucian's full line of sight. The man was visibly shaking and his expression was one Lucian had seen many times in his youth. Petulant anger. Where Lucian harnessed his, allowing adrenalin to make him more alert, Anders succumbed to rage and irrationality. And he was still that wilful, greedy child now, furious at being denied what he wanted. He'd been spoilt—Lucian knew it, because

Lucian had been spoilt too. And it took only a spark to set Anders's rage alight—to goad him beyond control. It was exactly what Lucian had expected—what he'd *wanted*—to happen. In front of the world.

'Please continue with your wedding, Anders,' Lucian said coolly.

'If you think I'm going to marry this frigid bitch now, you're crazy!' Anders snapped.

It wasn't a collective intake of breath this time, the entire congregation gasped in shock. Then there was a smattering of boos while a few people called out Anders's name in reproach. But the cretin stormed out of the cathedral. Not stopping to bow to Lucian as protocol dictated he should. Lucian didn't turn. He didn't savour the moment as he'd imagined he would so many times. He just watched the woman's face whiten and felt terrible.

'Get down. Give me that!'

The orders Anders gave to some hapless soldier outside the cathedral echoed within it. Then a cracking sound as a horse was whipped. More shouts.

She blanched.

No one would be able to deny what they'd just witnessed. Anders was cruel. Unfit to be King. He always had been. His jilted bride remained a single step away from Lucian, absorbing the murmurs and condemnation of the crowds. For the briefest moment she closed her eyes and the knife of remorse twisted inside him.

'I apologise for my cousin,' he said. 'He always lacked manners.'

'And yours are any better?' She barely moved her lips as she spoke in a response so soft that not even those amazing acoustics nor the myriad microphones would pick it up. It was a miracle Lucian heard it. But he did.

Was she angry with him? His gaze narrowed. Naive little fool. Surely she knew the rules of public life? There was a glimmer of pride in the way she kept her head high. The smattering he knew about her came back to him. She was the youngest princess of a much smaller realm across the Baltic that had removed all power from the royalty. She hadn't ever been on the social circuit, though she had two older sisters who were. Rumour had it her parents were desperately clinging to their regal nomenclature and still in denial about the disintegration of their aristocracy despite it being years since they were deposed. She'd met Anders only a couple of months ago. She might not appreciate it right now but Lucian had just done her a massive favour.

'May I have your permission to leave, Your Highness?' Chagrin glowed in her eyes but there was more than a glimmer of defiance too.

'Go with the bishop,' he muttered and nodded beyond the altar. 'That will give you more privacy.'

She turned her back on him and walked to the nave—her head high, those jewels still glittering. Lucian's gut twisted as he grimly watched her go. The bishop swiftly guided her to the small side door. In that sanctuary she could escape all the cameras. He would never see her again and that could only be for the good.

He waited until that side door closed before taking the last few steps to the altar himself. Then he turned to face the cathedral full of people. As he bowed before them he drew on that old, cold anger. It restored his determination and discipline. He would devote his life to becoming the King they deserved—to being better than the man he was. There would be no distraction, no decadence.

While providing heirs would be an imperative part of his future, he would not marry for a decade at least. He owed his country. Giving it his undivided attention for the duration that he'd been absent would ensure Monrayne was settled and secure. Even then his marriage would be a formal exercise, based on duty. He'd prioritised his private life in the past and he would regret it always. There was no room for personal indulgence, Monrayne would be his primary concern for ever, and of course the first item on his *to-do* list was to change the succession—Anders could not remain Crown Prince a moment longer than necessary.

He met Garth's rigid gaze. The fury that had accompanied him for what felt like all eternity coursed through his veins more strongly than ever.

'I am King Lucian of Monrayne,' he said clearly. 'And I am here to serve for as long as I live.'

CHAPTER THREE

Zara closed her eyes and tried once more to unfasten her wretched wedding dress. She'd managed to rip the veil from the intricate hairstyle but the rest—the bobby pins, the earrings and the millions of tiny buttons down her back were all too much. Contortionist she was not.

Hours had passed since those horrific moments in the cathedral in front of millions, in which her fiancé had brutally rejected her. Hours since Prince—*King*—Lucian Monrayne had returned from the dead.

The very distracted bishop had shown her to a tunnel and promptly abandoned her. To her amazement, the tunnel had emerged within the palace walls. After a couple of wrong turns she'd passed that portrait and finally found the suite she'd been staying in. Since then she'd been transfixed by the constant televised coverage. All those efficient palace assistants had vanished—presumably too fascinated by the return of the long-lost King to bother with an unwanted bride. She truly didn't blame them.

But while she'd appreciated the chance to be alone, she'd not expected it to be this long. Why hadn't her mother and sisters come to check on her—to take her home, even if it were to be in disgrace and mortification? She'd been rejected by her fiancé, dismissed from the King's presence and instantly forgotten by everyone. No one had knocked on the door in eons.

But then the world had plenty to occupy its collective mind. King Lucian's declaration at the front of the cathedral only moments after she'd left had been everything. It had been on repeat for hours and caught her attention every time it replayed—*he* caught her attention. Completely. In the cathedral when she'd stood before him the rest of the world had disappeared. All she'd been aware of was him—those ice-blue eyes, the scarred, angry, visceral strength of him. He was so cold. He'd been utterly expressionless as he'd personified the grenade which had decimated not just the day but obliterated the expected succession with a short couple of sentences.

Most of the foreign dignitaries had abruptly left. There was an endless series of private jets flying overhead, stoking an air of danger and political uncertainty. The world was agog with curiosity as to where Anders had fled. But the crowds outside the palace had continued to swell. Any citizens who'd not bothered to line the streets for Anders's wedding were now out in force for the return of Lucian. There was continuous chanting, cheers and revelry. It seemed the public were pleased.

The King had issued a statement asking everyone to go home and rest. That there would be formal televised announcements over the coming days, together with a full explanation of what had happened all those years ago and where he'd been for all of this time.

It didn't seem as if Garth had been altogether pleased to see Lucian, despite his acknowledgment of him. Zara's doubts about Anders intensified. She had the horrible feeling some of those more outlandish conspiracy theories about Lucian's disappearance all those years ago might not have been so outlandish after all.

So she really just wanted to get out of her dress now. Then out of here *entirely*. Though quite how she was going to do either, she didn't know. Even if she had been able to twist herself to undo the tiny buttons she couldn't because of the stupidly long nails the beauticians had insisted she wear to make the rings look nice. Nor could she cut the minuscule hand-stitching that seamstress had spent hours putting in. She was ready to scream with the frustration of it.

Thankfully, just then the door finally opened. But Zara's relief and appreciation died as she saw who strode in. Lucian himself.

The door slammed behind him and he'd taken only one step before he spotted her in the corner and abruptly halted. She watched him swiftly visually sweep the rest of the room before his gaze paused on the yards of silk tulle in a heap on the floor. His hands curled into fists.

The sight of him shocked her all over again, despite the fact he'd been emblazoned across the television screen for hours. He wasn't wearing his jacket but, to her immense relief, he'd put a top on. The black tee shirt ought to look incongruous with the formal trousers, yet somehow he pulled it off. It hugged his enormous muscles. He didn't look anything like a pampered Royal, more like an elite soldier. Or mercenary.

That was when her mind decided to replay the image of him standing bare-chested and statue-still in that cathedral. The light had shone down on him like some celestial intervention—highlighting the tattoo; the childhood scar on his ribcage; the tanned frame; his ridged abdomen; the dusting of hair on his chest that arrowed at his waistband. Ripped and raw, his was the hewn body of a fighter and every inch of it was imprinted on her mind—not budging even when she tried to blink it away.

She'd not seen her fiancé in such a state of undress. She'd not seen *any* man in such a state. Yes, she'd been that sheltered. She'd not even been allowed to bathe at public beaches. Not to protect her, not because she was that 'precious', but to help hide her family's drastically depleted resources. Her parents' pride wouldn't allow them to let her be seen in anything less than designer and, as they could afford none, then she couldn't be out.

Her older sisters had backed them up, adamantly insisting she remain in the countryside. She'd been stuck there so long she'd *almost* accepted it…until now.

'What are you doing in here?' He interrupted her thoughts with that arctic tone. 'Are you alone?'

Of course she was alone. She'd effectively been alone her entire life.

'What do you want?' His eyes narrowed. 'Why are you here?'

His accusatory tone made her hackles rise.

'This was the room I was assigned,' she said. 'I've been staying here for the last week.'

He didn't move, yet somehow he seemed even bigger. 'Once upon a time it was my room.'

She stared at him in horror. The man hadn't been home in who knew how long, for reasons also unknown, and she was in his room. Had she been sleeping in his *bed*?

'I wasn't aware of that. I apologise.'

She'd just been deposited here and left to her own devices and now she was utterly mortified. Again. But King Lucian showed no embarrassment. No emotion at all. He stepped closer, his gaze neutral. She almost shivered but she didn't want to betray her fear.

Except it wasn't fear making her shiver.

'I forgot you were…' He trailed off.

Right.

'Of course,' she muttered awkwardly. 'It's been a very busy time for you.'

Everyone had forgotten her. Especially him. Except the media chose that exact moment to remember her—airing the replay of Anders's rejection of her in the cathedral in that instant—

Frigid bitch.

She picked up the remote and turned the coverage off, but the insult echoed in the room. Somehow, she'd lived through that utter humiliation in front of millions, yet being alone with this particular man brought her anger forth now. He'd destroyed the day so clinically.

'If you could get someone to find me another room, I'll gather my things and go right away.' She turned towards the bedroom.

She heard his swiftly indrawn breath and next instant his hand landed heavily on her shoulder.

'What have you done?' he snarled huskily. 'You've hurt yourself.'

She froze at his touch. He must have moved *incredibly* swiftly.

'I haven't,' she choked.

'Your back is—'

'I can't get out of this dress,' she snapped. She was

already so mortified there was no point striving for any dignity now. 'I was a little thinner and they had to stitch me into it last-minute—' She broke off and twisted to face him.

His hand dropped but he was uncomfortably close now and he didn't back off. Nor did she. But there was fire in his eyes—a different kind of anger to the one she'd seen before.

'So you were trying to rip your way out of it and scratched yourself to pieces in the process?'

She hadn't scratched herself—or not as badly as he was suggesting.

'Where's your maid?' He glared at her.

She didn't actually have one. All those assistants had been supplied by the palace.

His expression tightened. 'What about your sisters? Your mother?'

'I don't know where any of my family is,' she mumbled.

He looked at her so intently she had the feeling he was holding something back from her.

'You should have been out of this get-up hours ago,' he said harshly.

'I agree.' She closed her eyes, refusing to cry. She'd been struggling alone for hours and suddenly she was hot and furious. The damned wedding dress made her skin crawl. She reached up behind her again to try to tug the back of the tightly stitched lace bodice apart.

'Stop hurting yourself.' He moved quickly, his hands encircling her wrists.

It brought him too close to her. No one had ever invaded her personal space like this. Her breathing quickened as he held her hands above her head. She felt a vulnerability that was absolute. He was so much stronger than her. But she also felt a sweeping yearning that was—

'You're badly marked,' he said huskily.

'I'm not,' she denied despairingly. She had zero pride left, zero strength to battle control on two fronts. So she just told him the truth. 'I get a rash when I'm upset or anxious, nervous, whatever. It looks worse than it is.' She drew a shaky breath. 'Hopefully, I haven't actually drawn blood. They'll kill me if I have—the dress is supposed to go on display later...'

There was a moment of awkward silence but she couldn't stop gazing up into his eyes. She could study that scar this close. It was a jagged, ugly mark that clearly hadn't been stitched by a skilled surgeon. It gave him a dangerous look. But his grip on her wrists was gentle. He smelled of caramel—a rich, sweet softness she'd not expected. She sensed he was holding himself rigid while within her all kinds of reactions were detonated. Weird ones. But ones she didn't quite want to end yet, which had to be why she remained so stupidly still.

'I will assist you,' he said gruffly, releasing her.

She shot him a startled look. 'You don't want to summon a maid and leave me to it?'

That serious expression didn't lighten. 'I am uncertain of which palace staff—if any—I can trust. I would prefer not to allow anyone else into this suite just yet.' His voice was a rusty monotone.

He was the most suspicious person on the planet. But then perhaps he had reason to be. She'd seen the footage of Anders's expression when he'd registered it was Lucian standing before him. And Garth's. Raw

shock had widened their eyes before undisguised horror burnished them. Ultimately ugly fury had contorted
Ander's entire stature. Lucian's return had been his
living nightmare.

So she nodded. Truthfully, she didn't want anyone
else to see her even more abandoned. This man had
seen her worst moment and he was more than enough.

'Well, if you wouldn't mind just cutting the back
of the dress where it's been stitched? Then I'll get out
of here and…'

She trailed off. She had no idea where she was going
to go or what she was going to do.

Impossibly, he was watching her even more closely
now. 'And…?'

She swallowed. 'I'm not sure.'

'No?'

She couldn't help hearing his cold tone as judgement. 'Gosh, it's not like I've been jilted at the altar
and humiliated in front of an audience of millions or
anything. I can't think why I would need some time to
get my head together.'

Anger flickered across his face. It pleased her,
oddly, to have forced a change in his plank-of-wood
impression.

'You may stay the night here while you work out
your plan for tomorrow,' he said stiffly.

'How very kind of you,' she said sharply. 'But if I
could just borrow a phone, I'll call my mother.'

'You have no phone?'

'Clearly not.'

His pale gaze flicked around the room again.

'There isn't one in here either,' she added.

His attention returned to her, yet she felt as if he'd

been aware of her every movement, every quickening breath all along.

And now he was even more stone-like. 'Unfortunately, your mother has already left.'

'What?' Her legs felt wobbly.

'Your sisters took her. They left in a jet two hours ago. Hitched a ride with the prime minister, I believe.'

'*What?*' How could he tell her this with such ambivalence? Her confusion grew. 'But you just asked me where they all were! Why did you do that if you already knew?'

His mouth tightened. Then he released a sharp breath. 'I wanted to see if you knew. If you'd chosen to remain deliberately.' His gaze travelled down her dress and his mouth tightened. 'Perhaps you didn't. But perhaps your mother wanted you to be stuck here.'

'Why would she want *that*?' Zara stared at him uncomprehendingly until her sluggish brain crawled to the most embarrassing conclusion. 'You don't think she wanted me to throw myself on your mercy?' She stared, aghast, at the obvious cynicism sharpening his gaze and spoke again before thinking. 'To throw myself at *you*?'

The thing was, it was exactly what her mother *would* want. She'd just have no faith that Zara would ever be capable of it. Rightly so, because Zara wasn't. She was appalled and ached unbearably at her family's rejection. The negative assumption of the man standing before her merely compounded the misery. She was *stupidly* hurt.

'A distasteful idea, I see.' A self-mocking smile flashed on his lips too briefly.

It was her mother's abandonment that was distasteful. Not, unfortunately, *him*.

'Do you think I am more dangerous to you than Anders?' he asked.

Yes. A million times *yes*.

Anders had never left her breathless. Or confused. Or questioning everything. Feeling oddly dizzy, she rubbed her forehead, trying to think and failing to ease the tension headache that had been building in intensity for hours. The diamond drop earrings on loan from the Monrayne vault were heavy. She wasn't used to wearing jewels like them. How had she ever thought she could carry off this performance? Because it was just a performance. A charade she'd tried to get through in order to make a better life. And yes, she couldn't get herself out of costume. She was stuck. Shamed. Unwanted and abandoned in a palace she couldn't escape.

Story of her life.

'You need assistance with those too, I see,' he muttered sardonically.

He leaned in, not giving her any space to escape. She was too surprised to step back anyway. She felt that warmth of him again—so at odds with his cool demeanour.

'Hold still,' he growled.

With slow care he removed one earring. Then the other. She held her breath the whole time. It seemed incongruous that this very large, lethally strong man who was clearly suppressing raging fury could be so gentle. Her heart thudded. He wasn't the charming-looking young prince of a decade ago. He was angrily ice-cold and ruthless and could easily hurt her. Yet she wasn't afraid. Because there'd been that moment in the cathedral where everyone had disappeared and she'd seen only him and he'd looked right back at her and maybe it was all in her head but she was sure something had passed between them. A recognition of emotion. Of understanding.

It happened again now. For a long moment she was lost in the depths of his eyes—like a crevasse in which she endlessly plummeted—until she blinked and inwardly cringed at her own flight of fancy. It would be so mortifying if he guessed what she was thinking.

'Better?' He sounded almost tender—but as if he cared?

She was mistaking quiet query for tenderness. And her, 'Thank you,' came out sharper than she intended.

He weighed the earrings in the palm of his hand and then set them on the low table near them. 'Why do you have your nails so long when you can't seem to do anything with them that length?'

'I don't usually. I bite them. These are fake.' Her whole look today was fake. 'My natural nails are so unsightly they had to be covered up.'

'Rendering you incapable at the same time?'

Because she wasn't used to them. She gritted her teeth. Did he have to point out the obvious quite so brutally? Did he have *no* heart—no compassion for her situation?

No. Compassion wasn't something this man would feel. He was too full of vengeance.

Yet she couldn't step away from him. Couldn't seem to do anything other than absorb his presence. Vital energy emanated from him with such intensity she couldn't understand *how* he had remained hidden for so long.

Suddenly her dress felt too tight. It ought to be her wedding night and here she was, being helped by the man who'd destroyed her day. Whose arrival had led to her absolute humiliation. And yet—she finally admitted to herself—she was more physically aware of him than she'd been of any other man in her life. She needed to get away from him and out of here. ASAP.

'Are you ever going to help me out of this dress?' she muttered impatiently.

'Are you ever going to turn around?'

CHAPTER FOUR

ZARA'S PULSE RACED and she frowned at him. 'Are you going to use your sword?'

'No.'

Was he going to shred her dress with his bare hands?

To her fascination—and horror—he swiftly retrieved a small dagger that was strapped to his ankle. 'I'm going to use this.'

The blade glinted. It was no ceremonial weapon. He'd concealed that he carried it. It was for real.

She shivered. 'You have that with you at all times?'

'This and more.' He looked at her directly. 'But I also know how to kill with my bare hands.'

She wasn't surprised and she knew he was trying to shock her. She *refused* to be intimidated.

'Yes, but my new nails might give you a run for your money.'

There was the slightest tightening at the corner of his mouth. 'If you were to push your thumbs into the eye sockets of an assailant then perhaps those nails could actually be useful.'

She swallowed. He wasn't smiling. He was perfectly serious.

'You should know how to take care of yourself,' he added.

The anger she'd kept at bay all afternoon seeped through her final defences. 'You don't think I already do?'

'No,' he said. 'You can't even seem to get yourself undressed.'

Seem? Did he *doubt* her struggles with this? Did he truly imagine that she'd been deliberately waiting for him to show up and strip her?

Perhaps your mother wanted you to be stuck here.

Didn't he believe that she'd been here with no idea that he'd walk in on her? Did he really think *she'd* tried to engineer this somehow?

The thing was, if Lucian had been the fiancé on offer in the first place, her sister Ana would have said yes in a heartbeat—even though he too was still younger than her. Because Lucian Monrayne hadn't just been gorgeous as a teenager, he'd been charming and intelligent and an all-round superstar.

Now fully grown, he was lethally attractive-looking. But he wasn't *charming* any more. He was hardened. Zara guessed he'd survived who knew what and, as a result, a sense of danger emanated from him. Yet he still stoked a different response within her. One that couldn't be more inappropriate. Angry about it, she pushed back, unable to restrain her curiosity.

'Why did you reveal yourself today?' she asked baldly.

He regarded her steadily and she knew he was deciding what—if anything—to reveal. He was irritatingly measured in his responses. Every word was considered and used sparingly.

'I required a public occasion for my return.'

He'd wanted a big show? Was that all?

'The coronation would have been even more public,' she pointed out.

'I didn't want to leave it that late,' he said with slow precision. 'I needed to ensure safety. For everyone. I needed time to ensure the coronation—'

'Was your own?' she interrupted as fierce emotion swamped her. 'And I was just collateral damage?'

His expression hardened. 'I wanted to stop the wedding,' he said. 'I wanted to rescue you from—'

'Did I *ask* you to rescue me?' she snapped.

His mouth thinned. 'You are disappointed.'

'*Disappointed?*' She should laugh.

He had no idea of what he'd done to her future. Suddenly all her anger was directed at *him*. 'You don't get to come here and leave me in a worse position than where I began.'

'Is that what I have done?'

'Of course it is. I've just been publicly humiliated by—'

'The man who was supposed to be in love with you. Not by *me*,' he pointed out coolly, but twin flames glowed in his eyes. 'You really wanted to marry him?'

'Well, I was standing in the church in a big white gown—'

'Because you're in love with him?'

She stilled, lost for words. Mortified, she remembered again how Anders had labelled her so cruelly. The reason for all her underlying, instinctive anxiety was finally clear. She'd known in her gut something wasn't right. But she'd been too desperate—too delusional about her future—to pay attention.

'It was a political arrangement,' she said, trying

to salvage her dignity. 'Mutually beneficial for both our nations.'

'Your *nations*?' he echoed sarcastically. 'Did you anticipate any *personal* benefits?'

She was an idiot for pursuing the idea in the first place. She'd thought she'd done something strategically clever. She'd even thought she'd managed to please her parents.

'I anticipated that I would have more personal freedom than what I've been accustomed to.'

She'd wanted respect too. She suspected now that she wouldn't have got either.

'Freedom?' he scoffed. 'And you were expected to provide an heir? Perhaps a spare as well?'

'Of course.'

'So, even though it was primarily a political arrangement, you were prepared to lie back and think of those other benefits?'

'I hadn't decided on the degree of intimacy I was willing to allow him.' She gritted her teeth. 'After all, there are methods other than the traditional for getting pregnant.'

He blinked and drew in a sharp breath. 'Indeed there are. Yet I can't imagine Anders agreeing to something so clinical. He's far more animal in his approach.' The words were ground from him. 'So you hadn't already slept with him.'

Her jaw dropped but, before she could snap back at him, he stepped closer.

'Had you kissed him?' Huskily, he asked more intrusive, more inappropriate questions. 'Have you kissed *anyone*, Princess?'

She held her ground, but only just. 'I don't see

what business that is of yours. Or what relevance it has to *anything*.'

'Because now here you are, with your untouched lips and untouched body, trying to get yourself into a barely dressed state for me to discover. Was that the new plan? To make yourself even more irresistible to me?'

Even more irresistible?

She gaped. The man was mad.

But he suddenly froze, his jaw angular. She just knew he would bite those words back if he could. The outrageousness of his accusation was incinerated by the heat she felt at that giveaway. But she wasn't going to let him *apologise* for admitting it. She was too busy trying to ignore her own inappropriate internal combustion.

Her pulse scurried. 'You're obviously overtired and stressed,' she said. 'That's the only explanation for your insanely rude assumptions. I never for a second imagined you were about to walk into this room and it's the height of arrogance to think that I would want... would want...'

'Me to touch you in any way?' he finished for her, his cool recovered. 'Yet isn't that just what you've asked me to do? Because apparently you need my help to get out of that dress. So turn around and I'll cut it off you.'

The *last* thing she wanted was his assistance now. And equally she knew it was the last thing *he* wanted to do now too. Which in all made her defiantly toss her head as she did as he'd commanded so savagely and turned her back on him.

There was a moment of stillness, yet her temperature soared as she felt the frisson of sexual promise that he surely hadn't meant. Then she felt his breath on the back of her neck. She closed her eyes, gritting her teeth so she wouldn't shudder in response. He carefully—far too slowly—worked the thin blade.

Her muscles screamed with the effort to stay still—not to lean back into him or to run away. Both urges were overwhelmingly intense. She'd never had a more intimate moment with any man. He was undressing her—or at least trying to. The flare of heat kept rising. She ached to be free of the confines of the horribly constricting dress. Her breasts felt crushed, her taut nipples ached. It was appalling. She needed his *help*. That was all. She didn't want anything *more*. Yet the drive deep within her was breathtakingly strong. And she just knew that he wasn't at all the cold-blooded warrior he appeared.

'Is it done?' she asked impatiently, embarrassed by her breathlessness. She couldn't stand to be this close much longer.

She heard a muttered imprecation beneath his breath, his control audibly weakening too.

'It's very tightly stitched,' he gritted.

'You can rip it to shreds for all I care.' She *desperately* needed to get away from him.

The second she felt it loosen she stepped forward for breathing space and—

'Wait—'

She heard a sharp shredding sound as she turned. A sudden coolness hit her skin. It was a blink before she realised the bodice had slipped to her waist.

He went rigid. 'Cover yourself.'

Her humiliation was overridden by a flare of fury unlike any other and, instead of doing as he ordered, she let her hands drop. It was in absolute defiance of everyone who'd told her what to do all day—what to do all her *life*. She was so sick of doing as she was told, trying to please, trying to be perfect, and failing. Her reason was obliterated in the heat of this last horror.

'*You* stood bare-chested in front of an entire *cathedral* of people, not to mention the millions watching on camera,' she spat. 'It means nothing. What does it matter if I'm bare-chested now?'

He'd already whipped the tee shirt over his head and now held it out to her. 'Put this on. Immediately. Or I'll put it on you myself.'

His gaze didn't waver from her eyes—not dropping to look at her half naked body again. He—unlike she—had too much self-control. She snatched the tee, turning away to put it on. It swamped her and was scented with that soft hint of sweet caramel and suddenly she was shaking. She held the skirts to her hips, shame and humiliation returning in a sweep. Yet she didn't entirely regret the flare. It had felt good to release just some of the fury.

But *he* flared now. 'You wore that dress for someone *else*.'

'I wore it for *myself*,' she said angrily. 'I was very deliberate in the style I agreed to. I wanted modesty to protect myself from their judgement, not to emphasise any impression of *innocence*.'

'In what possible way would they judge you negatively?'

She snatched a breath. 'Because I'm nothing like the perfect image presented today,' she muttered with a wobbly smile. 'Not just bitten nails. No one usually even sees me. But today I knew everyone would. So I went for the full makeover. I'm covered almost head to toe in diamonds and silk and lace to distract from what's beneath.'

'Why would you desire to distract anyone from what's beneath? I've just seen——' He bit his lip and didn't finish the sentence.

She wanted him to finish it. She wanted so many wild, impossible things. Most of all—right now—his touch. She wanted to lose herself in the overwhelming masculinity, the strength, the sensual drive emanating from him. She wanted him to sweep her away. It was absolutely insane.

He stepped away, only to suddenly swing back. 'You were the first to acknowledge that I was who I said I was. We have not met. What made you so sure?'

'Your eyes.' She answered automatically.

He said nothing.

'The colour,' she added in a mumble. 'The shape.'

'Despite the scar?'

'Of course.' She couldn't look away from him. She was almost overcome by the desire to trace the gap in his eyebrow with the tip of her finger. 'Did you get it——?'

'When I nearly died? Yes.'

'Was it…?'

'Anders who tried to finish me off? Yes. Not only had you not slept with him, you barely knew him. You may not like to hear it, but I *did* rescue you from far more than you realise.'

She glared at him, hoisting her dress again with her hands on her hips. 'Really?'

Her movement made him glance down. Now he stared at her hand and his voice was very soft. 'You are probably equally unaware that the ring you wear once belonged to my mother.'

Her anger evaporated. She wanted to die. Right now. She couldn't breathe as she tried to get it off her finger while still trying to hold her skirt up, but it was a desperate disaster. 'Please take it back. Please. I don't want it.'

'If you'll stop panicking and stand still for half a second, I'll do just that,' he snapped.

They both stilled. He was breathing as hard as she now. Both of them a whisper away from loss of control. But that intimacy resurged as he carefully worked the ornate ring from her finger. His scent enfolded her, his heat, his shocking gentleness, and her emotions were on the biggest rollercoaster—she was *not* going to cry in front of this man.

At last he held the ring and she stepped back. The precious stones glinted in the light.

His expression became that stark mask again. 'I came here to stop Anders's marriage because I know what lies beneath his facade. You're not collateral damage and you may now return to your home.'

'I *may*.' She echoed his patronising permission. 'What if I don't wish to return home?'

Why would she ever want to return there now?

His expression shut down. 'I have no desire nor need for a wife at present.'

She gaped. 'Do you *seriously* still think I'm here to offer myself to you? That I would go from one groom to another in a single afternoon?'

But the awful thing was, she *was* attracted to him. It was very sudden. Very strong. And she was trying so, *so* hard not to stare at his magnificent chest.

There was a slight twist of his lips, *almost* a smile. 'Well, what am I to think when I find you attempting to undress yourself in my bedroom…?'

'You're to think that I was being honest when I told you this room was assigned to me. That I've been staying in here all week.'

All week while she'd been alone—ignored by her prospective groom and her family.

'But you're not sure who—if anyone—is honest, are you?'

His expression shut down again. 'You no longer need to sacrifice yourself for family or country.'

'I chose to accept the engagement to Anders,' she said proudly. 'It was *my* decision. It wasn't forced upon me by my greedy family, if that's what you're thinking. I didn't need you to rescue me. I was here on my own terms with my eyes wide open.'

'Is that right?' he said with soft sarcasm. 'Because you knew your fiancé so well. You knew all about his particular preferences.'

She swallowed, unsure of what he meant but understanding at least that it was something ugly.

'And would an arranged, passionless marriage really have fulfilled you?' he added with a glint in his eye. 'Didn't you want more?'

Zara hadn't wanted to admit that Anders's crude insult had hit so hard mostly because she'd feared it might be true. At least regarding him.

'There are other things that lead to fulfilment,' she said obstinately. 'A physical relationship is not always necessary.'

'What if you'd fallen in love with someone else?'

'How was I going to meet someone to fall in love

with? My lifestyle doesn't lend itself to finding lovers easily.'

She'd been cloistered in the castle in the country all through her childhood, slowly taking on more and more care of her ageing parents while being told over and over by her sisters how much life there suited her—that she was lucky because she was too shy and too awkward to enjoy working in the city.

'Well, now you are free to do as you wish,' he said stiffly.

'*Free?*' she said bitterly. 'You do not understand the perilousness of my position.' It was appalling. 'My lack of *preciousness*. I am a third-born princess who—'

'Do you really think your only value is your virginity on your wedding night?' he interrupted harshly. 'What century do you think this is?'

'Well, by everyone's calculations it seems I have little else to offer.'

'I too am a virgin, yet I find I still have plenty else to offer,' he growled.

'You—' She broke off, utterly shocked and unable to believe what she'd just heard. Yet in the next breath she did. 'You don't feel that need?'

There was a moment of mortifying silence in which she then couldn't believe she'd asked that.

Lucian Monrayne struck her as a man who'd take what he needed whenever he needed it. And somehow—with his size, his imperiousness—he seemed like he'd need a lot. Her mouth dried.

'Do you?' he eventually countered coolly.

Her heart skidded. Until today she'd have said she didn't. Anders's barb had struck home and she was certain Lucian was thinking of those cruelly thrown words too.

She squared her shoulders and lifted her chin. 'No. I don't.'

His scarred eyebrow lifted and she felt her face flush. But surely this *frisson* inside her right now was an aberration—shock or something.

'Whether or not I do is irrelevant because I have too much work to do. I suggest you find *your* work,' he advised bluntly. 'Then get on with it.'

'I don't need you to *mansplain* my options to me.' She was angry and insulted and *fascinated*. 'Perhaps I never had the opportunity to be *educated* for any real work in the way that you did,' she said. 'There was no exclusive boarding school for Royals for *me*.'

Lucian had been sent to one, she knew. So had her sisters. They'd all had an elite education abroad, just perfect for young Royals. But Zara had been unexpectedly conceived more than a decade after Ana's birth and by the time she was old enough for that school her parents had been banished to the castle.

'There was only house arrest for me. My parents wanted to hide their financial mismanagement and were too proud for me to be seen going to an ordinary school in ordinary clothes.'

'They kept you at home?'

Mia and Ana had been in their twenties by then. Even though they were powerless princesses, they were well-educated, well-connected and adaptable and still became social darlings. Neither had the time to deal with their parents. That was Zara's role.

'I was fortunate enough to have a governess.' She shot him a look.

'A governess?' His eyebrow lifted crookedly. 'For all this time?'

'I've been caring for my parents and helping run the castle since finishing what education I was offered.'

Even as she'd got older her sisters had leaned upon her to stay there. She was needed at home and 'so good' at managing her parents' demands. And she was too 'shy', too 'awkward' to want to go to university or to work in the city. But that was only because she'd never had the practice, the chance to get used to it or grow in confidence.

For so long she'd believed them—part of her still did. She'd been cast as the shy youngest, 'happy' to live in seclusion. In truth, she'd effectively been stranded in the countryside, caring for parents who couldn't have cared less whether she was there or not. In the end her resentment at having her life suppressed by the assumptions and expectations of her family had grown.

She stiffened at the thought of it all now. 'So when Garth came to visit—'

'*Garth* approached you?' Lucian interrupted.

'My sister Ana. She said she was too old for Anders.'

'So you stepped in?'

'Yes.'

'Had you even *met* Anders at that point?' His frown deepened as she shook her head. 'What was so awful that you needed to escape?'

She paused. How could she explain it to *him,* given all he'd been through? Her discomforts paled in comparison in terms of trauma and isolation. Yes, she'd been stuck in her ramshackle castle, yes, she'd been emotionally neglected, but at least she'd been physically safe, whereas Lucian had been in the wilderness for a decade. Declared dead. *Wanted* dead.

'I thought it was an opportunity for a better life,' she explained weakly. 'But it seems he was only interested in my enthusiasm to give him my innocence and even that in itself had to be *proven*—'

'Before he'd take you as his bride?' Lucian finished harshly. 'Yes, that sounds very like Anders. Given his depraved proclivities, I don't think he was going to accept your idea of some alternative method of impregnation.' Lucian said. 'I think you should consider yourself lucky that Anders walked out of the wedding.'

'I should consider myself lucky that I was publicly humiliated all over again, after already enduring that medical exam?' she asked bitterly.

'He would have humiliated you in far worse ways than that, had the marriage gone ahead,' he said unfeelingly. 'So isn't it fortunate I turned up when I did?'

She stared at him, exasperated. But his scent and warmth and proximity confused her all over again and she suddenly had the most absurd urge to fall in and let him embrace her—as if he'd ever do that. This man had returned for his Crown and had no compunction about doing whatever was necessary to restore his rights. He was also wildly arrogant about it.

So she lifted her chin and made herself take a step backwards. 'I apologise for my apparent lack of gratitude,' she said. 'It's been a very confusing day.'

'I also apologise,' he replied roughly. 'You're in a vulnerable position. Get some sleep. It won't seem so bad in the morning.'

She gritted her teeth yet again. She *really* didn't

want his patronising reassurance. That was when she saw the glimmer of a smile in his eyes.

'You disagree, Princess?'

Honestly, she completely disagreed. She'd been publicly jilted. Her family had left without her. She'd been accused of trying to entice the new King—by the new King himself, who was infuriatingly attractive.

He was also determinedly self-sufficient. She paused. The man was obviously an absolute survivor. Which was what she now needed to be. So maybe she could learn a few things from him.

As if he would allow that. He had so much else to be getting on with. And now she felt absurdly melancholic. In all likelihood, she would never see him again.

'I can't sleep in here,' she grumbled. 'It's your suite.'

'It has not been mine for so very long that one more night will make little difference.' He turned and walked away from her. 'I'll ensure someone attends to you first thing and gets you wherever you would like to go. Goodbye, Princess.'

CHAPTER FIVE

LUCIAN STEPPED INTO the corridor, released a tightly held breath and tried to summon self-control. He'd had only a few moments to himself before another meeting and hadn't expected to spend them stripping someone else's bride and trading lack of sexual histories with her. It had been *madness*. But he'd been unable to resist. In truth, that was the longest private conversation he'd had with another person in ages and, to his amazement, he'd enjoyed it. The little princess who'd usurped his bedroom was surprisingly forthright and feisty and now he needed a moment because his response to her had become *intense*.

Initially he'd thought he might learn something useful from her. While it seemed unlikely she was a confidante of Anders, given his ungallant outburst in the cathedral, his cousin could pull off a bluff better than anyone. So Lucian had held back the information about her mother and then watched closely for her reaction when he'd finally informed her. She'd been utterly transparent—humiliated, hurt and hopelessly honest.

She *hadn't* been waiting to greet him in that stunning redundant wedding gown. And the bluntness with which she'd admitted her 'flaws'—that her appearance was as fake as her nails; that she'd undergone a make-over to pretend to be a perfect princess; that she'd actually thought everyone was looking at her *dress* and not the delectable form beneath it or the beautiful depths of her eyes, all confirmed his gut impression that she was utterly naive. If he had a heart he'd consider it endearing. Instead, it infuriated him. How could Garth have ever considered her to be an appropriate match for Anders?

Furthermore, it infuriated him that she was still here. Because *his* reaction to her was infuriating. It had been from the first.

In the cathedral, in that moment when he'd finally been about to confront Anders face to face, he'd been blinded by her beauty. But now he'd discovered that beneath that cloudy veil and glittering jewels was no perfect princess at all. She was so much better—imperfectly *genuine*—and he'd been compelled to get closer still. It was shocking. But he reasoned that his awareness of her was just a base reaction because of his entirely stressed-out state. He was operating on pure adrenalin and *all* his senses were hyperalert. So this intensely physical response was merely an outlet for some of the pressure of this whole situation. It wasn't *real*. If he ever saw her again in the future he'd likely feel little. Because ordinarily he felt little for anyone.

His emotional bonds had been destroyed in the aftermath of his 'accident'. His cousin's betrayal was bad enough but his mother's death so soon after had devastated him completely and he'd resolved to remain focused on his duty first and for ever.

Because it was his fault that she'd died alone and heartbroken. His fault that he and Anders had been on that boat in the first place. Because he'd been a selfish, petulant teen who'd wanted time to himself, a holiday, leaving his mother alone when she'd needed him most.

His loyalty to his friend, King Niko of Piri-nu, was the last true bond that remained from his past. They'd met at school—one of those elite institutions that apparently Zara hadn't been allowed to attend. They'd been proud alpha princes, battling each other for academic and sporting supremacy and becoming best friends in the attempt. It had been Niko who'd saved his life after the accident when, injured and in hiding, Lucian had sent him coded word. But while Lucian would feel indebted to Niko for ever, he'd repaid him all he could in time and service. Now Monrayne needed all his attention.

He huffed out another breath to push away the ache that princess had left him with. Then he hunted down a servant and demanded they provide the princess with a phone and food first thing and then make whatever travel arrangements she wanted.

At last he returned to the courtiers who'd gathered in the throne room. The assorted dignitaries attending the wedding had rapidly left Monrayne. He wasn't offended. Given there was a chance of upheaval and civil unrest following his wholly astonishing return, he too would've advised anyone who wasn't a citizen to leave. Just in case. Which was why it was shocking to him that Princess Zara had been so abandoned by her family. And if she'd not been properly educated or able to enter society then no wonder she'd wanted to escape her home so completely.

But he knew it was safe enough for her to stay the night for there would be no constitutional crisis here.

While the media was still in a frenzy, the swelling crowds at the gate were calm—holding candles and alternating between chanting his name and singing the national anthem. Their continued celebrations took him aback, as did the fact they were calling his return a miracle. Lucian just felt all the more guilty. He should have returned sooner. But he'd owed Niko and he'd needed to wait for the right time.

Anders's disappearance now was yet more proof of his nature. But he would be detained the second he emerged from whatever rock he was hiding beneath. He was too greedy to survive long without the luxury and excess he was used to. He was also too arrogant to believe he was in any real danger. But the fact was Lucian was the least of his threats, for without his protection officers Anders would be more vulnerable to the wrath of the criminal figures he'd tangled with in recent years.

Lucian's immediate duty had to be to stabilise his country. He didn't fear for his own safety now he was here and recognised. It wouldn't take long to secure the new succession plan so there was no chance of Anders taking the Crown, even if the worst were to happen. He dealt with Garth swiftly. Both sycophantic and defensive, the man actually offered his services. Lucian made him surrender his diplomatic passport and papers and then had him escorted to his apartment, where he would remain under guard. Tempting as it was to toss him straight into the palace dungeons, he didn't. There would be a trial for fraud. Until then, house arrest. Lucian would do things by the book.

It was only a few hours from dawn when he finally called a halt to the meetings. He slowly walked through the tunnel, returning to the cathedral—this time going down the stone steps and using the heavy iron key to unlock the family crypt.

His father had died so long ago Lucian barely remembered him, but he'd loved his mother. He pressed his hand against the cold stone that marked her resting place and bowed his head as remorse devastated him. Anders had caused so much hurt to a woman who had already lost so much. To a woman who'd offered him only welcome. But Anders had only been able to do that because of Lucian. The accident had been Lucian's own fault.

He'd been selfish. He'd known she was unwell but he'd pushed to go on his precious 'holiday' anyway. He'd left her alone when she was vulnerable. And she'd died believing him to be dead. At that moment he almost had been. He'd been fighting for his life in a battle with pneumonia on the other side of the world in Pirinu. If he'd only done as she'd first asked, if he'd simply done his duty, then he wouldn't have been on that boat with Anders and his mother wouldn't have died so much sooner than she ever should have.

So now, as he bowed his head, he offered his apologies silently. But he could never forgive himself for it. He could only vow to do better. He would give his country the decade of service he'd denied it—his undivided, complete attention. He would become the monarch his country deserved and honour his mother's legacy at last.

Eventually he returned to his old wing and took a room that had once been reserved for his servant. But he couldn't sleep. Memories tormented him. Such betrayal. Such bitterness.

But suddenly *new* memories stole in—ones infinitely preferable to the usual nightmares. He closed his eyes and breathed deep—hearing Princess Zara's soft gasp as he'd stood too close to her; feeling her slender wrists and the warmth of her sensitive, silken skin with its patchwork of pink and scarlet; the curve of her breasts had made his mouth water. He hadn't touched anyone in a long time and her skin was tantalisingly soft. His body ached *hard*.

But Lucian couldn't let desire consume him. He had too much to do. He threw back the bedclothes and strode to the shower.

Hours later he stalked into the small dining room. He needed food and he needed a moment away from the suited, wide-eyed courtiers, police representatives and politicians. But he froze in the doorway, struggling to suppress his reaction as he registered who was seated at the polished table. The rush of revitalising energy was undeniable. It was as if she were a portable power pack. One that all but electrocuted his brain.

He grimly shook the paralysis off and stepped forward. Her face grew impossibly paler before flushing in a swathe of scarlet blotches. Once more she clearly hadn't expected his arrival.

'I didn't realise you were still here,' he muttered before thinking. 'And I certainly didn't expect to find you in my private dining room.'

He'd told that servant to attend to her properly. Perhaps her plane out of here was delayed?

'I didn't realise this is your private dining room,' she hissed indignantly. 'This is just where they put me to feed me.'

Yet she hadn't done all that much eating, had she?

He sat opposite her and took in the vast untouched array of breads, salads and sliced meats separating them. He didn't feel like eating any of it either. He'd not given a public speech in a long time and there were going to be millions watching him this afternoon. Analysing every word. Words he still hadn't written.

He poured himself a strong coffee and sat back to study her. To his utterly inappropriate pleasure, she stared right back at him. In the resulting silence he realised he was absurdly amused. He ought to be working—he faced endless meetings, apologies, information to absorb, questions, diplomatic visits and decisions... not to mention that speech ahead of him in less than an hour. He needed this time to collect his thoughts. Instead, he succumbed to the urge to let her disturb his few moments of respite—making them a delight.

Those ridiculous talons had gone and, sure enough, her natural nails were bitten to the quick, unpolished and frankly painful-looking. She wore a high-necked jumper as if trying to hide the skin that gave her emotions away, but he could still see the blotchy colour at the neckline. The perfect princess in the cathedral had definitely been aided by make-up, diamonds and lace coverings. Good for her. Yet now she looked too young, too defenceless, and suddenly that cold anger resurged from deep within. For a man filled with regret, he had none about destroying her wedding ceremony. Not a single one. Anders would have been cruel. He would have destroyed *her*.

'Can we get some fresh fruit, please?' he finally glanced away and requested from the warily hovering servant. 'Unpeeled and uncut.'

He wanted to bring the sparkle back to her eyes and banish the flicker of hopelessness that dulled them.

'Did you get *any* sleep?' she asked in a low voice once the servant had left the room.

Was that her way of telling him he looked as terrible as he felt?

'Did you?'

'The crowds kept calling for you all through the night.' That colour washed her skin again. 'And you've been busy.' She gestured to the headlines on a tablet she had in front of her instead of food. 'Garth's been arrested for financial mismanagement. Anders appears to have banished himself.'

Lucian stiffened. 'I'll be happier when he's found and faces justice.'

'You're looking for him?'

'Of course.' He hadn't brought a large team with him, but he had people looking now. It wouldn't be long before Anders surfaced.

'You wanted to take him down in the most public way possible,' Zara said. 'You say that was for safety, but you can't deny there wasn't an element of revenge in there. You wanted to see the look in his eyes as he realised exactly who you were, and you wanted the rest of the world to see it too. You wanted to provide incontrovertible proof of his true nature to the world.'

He spread his hands. 'Does that make me a monster?'

She shook her head. 'No. It was the choice you made.'

'What other choice was there?'

'To come back sooner?' She regarded him carefully. 'Why did you stay away so *long*?'

The question burned. He would have to explain exactly this to his nation shortly.

'You sound angry about it.'

'If you'd come back sooner this mess with Anders wouldn't have happened. I wouldn't be in this position. I wouldn't have had to—'

'It's quite amazing how you can turn all of this into my fault,' he said thoughtfully. 'Are you saying you wouldn't have considered marrying Anders if he weren't going to be King?'

She stiffened. 'You make me sound calculating. It wasn't like that. I wasn't being entirely selfish.'

He didn't actually think she was. In fact, he felt a tug of understanding. Things were invariably more complicated than they appeared—like his reasons for being gone so long. Zara didn't know he hadn't been well for a long time. That he'd gone through not one but two near-death experiences—the accident itself and then pneumonia only days later. Nor did she know he still wasn't *good* enough to take the Crown—he was only here because he was a better option than Anders. But he was hardly about to tell her all of that.

'My physical recovery after the accident took some time,' he explained briefly. 'I made it to Piri-nu and convalesced there. But my mother died before learning I was safe. The situation in Monrayne then became complicated.'

He'd not had health or strength or money. He'd been utterly powerless to take on Garth at eighteen. But he was never going to be in that position again. He would ensure Monrayne's stability and his own strength.

'Ten years is a *long* time,' she said.

'I had to wait until the time was right.'

'Is all this horrible stuff about Anders true?' She gestured to the news articles on the screen. 'Or is it a smear—part of the campaign to restore faith in you? Have your people been leaking stories all night?'

He read a few of the more salacious headlines upside down.

'The media reports have nothing to do with me.' He glanced up and that hardness inside eased a little at the concern in her eyes. 'And what you read there is all true. It's not even half of it,' he added. 'Anders routinely gorged on drugs, drink and enjoyed exerting power over unwilling women.'

Her face flushed. 'How could I not have known that?'

'Because until last night Garth had control of the media.'

Her eyes widened. 'And now you do?'

'No. Now there is a *free* press. I'll not allow that corruption to continue. I'll not be a dictator.'

'Why did no one warn me? Surely people must have known something—or suspected? Why would Garth let me…?'

That had been another source of his anger.

'Perhaps he thought that Anders wouldn't dare harm you, given your status. Or his own greed blinded him to the depths Anders had sunk. I think he was arrogant enough to believe he could control him.'

She stared at him in horror. 'I get that you needed to gather your strength. But surely that didn't take a decade.'

'I needed to accumulate all kinds of resources for my return. Niko had done too much for me already. I couldn't ask for more assistance.'

'King Niko of Piri-nu?' She regarded him thoughtfully. 'It says online that you worked in his security team.'

'He saved my life,' he said harshly. 'I owed him.'

'So you repaid him with loyalty and time?'

He nodded. 'I also needed the opportunity. I couldn't fail and I couldn't leave *any* room for doubt. I needed the eyes of the world upon Monrayne in that moment I returned. There could be no risk of violence. No one else could be hurt.'

'At least not physically,' she muttered.

He paused. 'Right.'

She stared down at the headlines again. 'I never would have resented my *rescue* if I had known about this.'

'Is that your way of saying "thank you" at last?'

She glanced back up and there was a sad smile in her eyes. 'I'm not afraid to say the words, but only when they're warranted.'

'Are they not now?' He inclined his head. 'Are you still angry with me for interrupting the wedding? He would have enjoyed forcibly removing that dress from you, Zara. He'd have done it with far more violence than I did, and he'd have done far worse once he had.' His tension built until he sighed in frustration. 'You should go back to your family.'

Her expression grew pinched. 'My family didn't wait for me. They won't be interested in how I'm *feeling*. They'll want me to hide in that castle like a pariah princess for the rest of my life. I'll be scorned and shamed.' She shook her head. 'I'm not exactly raring for that to happen.'

He could help her disappear. Get her a new name, a

new identity. But he knew how lonely that life was and his gut told him that wasn't right for her.

'So you don't wish to return home.' He glanced at another of the headlines on the screen. 'At least sympathy is on your side.'

'*Sympathy.*' She grimaced. 'Well, isn't that just all I've *ever* wanted?'

Zara watched Lucian pull his dagger and begin peeling an apple from the bowl of fruit the servant had brought in.

Pity wasn't something this cold, clinical man would indulge in. Nor was pleasure, apparently. His claim of virginity still shocked her, yet it also made sense. She suspected self-discipline mattered to him. Proving his self-control. He'd apparently been so patient—biding his time as he'd focused on only one thing—was it revenge?

He'd spoken of his time in banishment, of his mother's death and of his physical recovery with zero emotion. But there'd been loyalty to Niko, the King of Piri-nu. She'd heard of that beautiful Pacific Island nation of course. She suspected Niko meant more to him than merely being the King he owed. He was Lucian's friend—which meant he must be less of a block of ice sometimes.

Now he sat there peeling more of the wretched fruit with skilled, swift precision. He was silent, predatory, *lethal*. Yet she wasn't afraid of him. Her current adrenalin boost wasn't based on anxiety.

The realisation that her family had been all too willing to accept her sacrifice churned her innards. Surely her sisters *must* have heard whispers about Anders, given they were so socially connected back in Dolrovia? But even if they hadn't—even if they were as oblivious as she'd been, shouldn't they have stayed after that horror in the cathedral to ensure she was safe? She was beyond hurt that they'd simply abandoned her. But her mother was probably still deluding herself that they were some grand, important family and thus had needed to escape quickly. She would now be watching Lucian with eagle eyes.

'My mother is probably hoping you'll honourably save my mortification by marrying me yourself,' she mused morosely.

'No,' he responded instantly and uncompromisingly. 'That wouldn't be honourable. Besides which, I won't marry for years.'

Yeah? Well, she wasn't going to marry *at all* now. She'd thought it would be the solution to her problems once and she couldn't have been more wrong. Lesson learned. But she was momentarily diverted. 'You have no desire to secure the succession of *your* lineage?' She suddenly smiled. 'Oh, no. No desire at all, I forgot.'

'I have as little desire in me as you do, Sweet Princess.' He sliced the apple clean through and offered her a piece. 'Don't worry, I've begun the process to ensure Anders cannot take the Crown. Some other distant cousin will inherit if I die before having heirs of my own. But I won't be marrying anyone for a decade at least. I need to focus fully on Monrayne and I would never risk bringing children into this tumultuous time.'

He was so very serious and controlled, it annoyed her.

Taking the apple slice, she cocked her head. Periodic cheering could still be heard in the streets.

'Doesn't sound that tumultuous to me. They're out there celebrating.'

He lifted his head coolly. 'So you think—'

'That your marriage and subsequent children would only bring *more* security to Monrayne.' She couldn't resist provoking him a little. 'So perhaps, for your people, you ought to do that sooner rather than later.'

'Absolutely not,' he said softly. 'Not—'

'For as long as possible?' she finished softly.

'Exactly.' Implacable and definite, he clearly had a plan and was sticking to it.

His cold, measured certainty was both compelling and aggravating. What if he met someone amazing and fell instantly in love—would he still not marry for a 'decade at least'?

He returned to the task of peeling and slicing the apple. He offered every other slice to her. It was oddly intimate, though she was quite sure that he didn't intend it that way. But the gesture gave her the excuse to keep watching him.

She hadn't thought it possible for him to be better-looking but, even with the ravages of a clearly sleepless night and the weight of a nation on his broad, broad shoulders, he was gorgeous. Yes, it hadn't been those noisy crowds outside that had kept *her* awake all night.

'Where are you going to go?' he eventually asked.

Unlike him, she didn't have an eight-point plan perfectly formulated—*yet*.

'Where do you suggest?' she asked a little bitterly. 'A friend? There's none of those. My family, who abandoned me in their haste to ensure their own safety? Never. And with what money shall I make my escape? Where was I supposed to go when I left the cathedral, trapped in an enormous dress that I couldn't escape? So—' she counted the failings off on her fingers '—no funds, no friends, no family, no car, no clothes, no… I've got nothing.' She shrugged. 'Maybe my marriage might not have been ideal, but at least I had some kind of plan—'

'With a psychopath.'

'Maybe I would have had palace support,' she muttered valiantly. 'I would have had time to figure something else out once I'd realised.'

'You have no idea of the danger you were in.'

'Maybe not then, but I do realise that I'm *still* in danger of a sort *now*. I can't go back to my life as it was. It doesn't exist any more anyway. I'll always be the frigid, jilted non-princess now. I need time to figure it out, otherwise I'll end up trapped again and being told what I can and can't do.'

He glanced up from the apple. 'So what's your solution?'

She held her breath in a last attempt to bring inner calm, but then just blurted it out. 'People are selfish. Most people, in fact. Even you. So *I'm* going to be selfish. You're not getting rid of me. I'm staying here.'

He stopped peeling the apple entirely. 'Pardon?'

'I'm staying. Here. Just for a little while longer.' She pressed her lips together.

'And if I say no?'

'You wouldn't want to be seen as ruthless and uncaring,' she said. 'Because if you said no, then I would have no choice but to walk out the front gates in my shredded wedding dress and tell the world that the King of Monrayne abandoned me in my hour of need. Shamed again.'

His ice-blue eyes remained trained on her. 'Are you blackmailing me?'

'I guess that could be one interpretation.'

'You realise I could truss you up and have you on a flight out of here in less than ten minutes? And I could do that with one hand tied behind my back—'

'And no doubt blindfolded as well,' she added drolly. 'But you won't.'

'No?'

'No. You don't want anyone hurt. You want your country safe. You need to be well regarded for that to happen.'

He looked at her a second longer and then his attention dropped to the half-decimated apple. 'I suppose I could inform your family that you've gone to a private sanctuary. Buy you some time to sort your life out.'

'A private sanctuary?'

Was he going to send her away? Oddly, that wasn't what she wanted at all.

But, of course, he had far bigger things to be concerned with than some lowly princess who had no riches, no real kingdom and no real purpose. Of course he didn't want her to remain under his actual roof.

'Do you mean like a spa or something?' She tried to summon enthusiasm and appreciation. 'A luxury health retreat?'

'No. That would just be the cover for you staying here. Despite the fact that if I so much as sneeze it will be reported on, you can likely hide best right here behind the palace walls.'

Stupidly relieved, she popped another piece of apple into her mouth to hide her smile.

'Just for a day or so,' he added, still watching her

closely. 'Please yourself, Princess. Rely on no one. *Count* on no one.'

'Is that your mantra?' She regarded him curiously. She didn't believe that she couldn't count on *him*. He'd helped her multiple times already and, honestly, she was considering asking him for even more. She didn't particularly want to—but what she'd said was true. She had nothing. Would he consider giving her a loan, perhaps? So she could upskill and get an actual job. She'd pay him back with any interest he wanted. But having just secured his permission to stay a couple more days, she decided now wasn't the time to push for more. Especially when he seemed determined to keep his distance.

'You can have full freedom within the palace.' He ignored her question. 'I'll be busy so our paths are unlikely to cross. If there's more you need, ask Victor, the new servant.'

He didn't want to be bothered by her. Of course, why would he when he had an entire kingdom to restore? Yet she couldn't help feeling slightly piqued.

'May I? Thank you so much.'

He paused peeling yet another apple and focused his attention on her again. 'You want more from me?'

Some vestige of emotion? An iota of humanity— of heat? What she *really* wanted was…*not appropriate*. She froze as she realised that truth, staring at him while desperately fighting off the sudden yearning inside. The silence thickened. His ice-blue eyes were suddenly hot and awareness of his mounting tension rippled through her.

She put down her apple slice. 'I appreciate your patience in putting up with me. I know I can be…'

To her astonishment, a smile suddenly flickered on his face. She was so surprised she couldn't finish her sentence.

'What do others say you can be, Zara?' he prompted softly.

A disappointment. An annoyance. A drain on resources. But this was a man who'd survived an assassination attempt. She couldn't complain to him more than she already had in the last few minutes. That would be too pathetic.

'It doesn't matter.' She shook her head. 'I promise I'll be good. Quiet. You won't even know I'm here.'

He studied her even more intently and she felt that sensual awareness bloom anew.

'I won't know?' He regarded her consideringly. 'Do you equate being good with being quiet?' he asked slowly. 'Because that's not appropriate in all situations.'

Tension simmered as she stared at him. Was that *innuendo* from the virtuous King? He was too measured, too considered for it *not* to be deliberate. But—

'I would be very disappointed if you were silent, Princess.'

Her mouth dried. 'Sometimes survival is dependent upon silence.'

'True,' he agreed. 'But, equally, sometimes it's dependent upon screaming.'

He meant for help. He didn't mean in some sexual way. Only that wasn't how her brain was interpreting it. She stared at him.

'I guess the trick is knowing when to employ which option.'

CHAPTER SIX

ZARA DIDN'T SEE the King for three days. Well, not in the flesh. She saw plenty of him on screen. She watched his speech. Watched the footage of him emerging from meetings with politicians and the elite. Watched the endless repeats of those moments in the cathedral. His progress was swift and dramatic. The plans for the coronation were delayed until the dust had settled as he focused on steering the nation through the change smoothly, but indeed it was a swift, bloodless restoration. King Lucian of Monrayne—with his undisputed lineage—reclaimed the throne utterly unopposed.

The crowds kept cheering. Zara watched constant deliveries of letters, cards and gifts. Political pundits and social media opinion writers commented on the vast change from smiling, personable young man to remote, solemn king. They were saddened by his lack of smiles and the obvious physical trauma he'd endured, despite his incredibly strong physique now.

The murky truth of that fateful day was analysed over and over. The official report had always been that Lucian and Anders had been on a summer holiday in the Mediterranean. They'd gone out on a small vessel to go diving. Lucian had gone overboard and hit his head. Anders had been in shock and struggled to raise the alarm. The boat with Anders wasn't found for hours and Lucian's body never recovered in the intense searches in subsequent weeks. Lucian's mother had rapidly declined in the immediate aftermath and died only days later. It seemed her cancer had been kept secret from the public. It had all been a dreadful tragedy.

But now there were other whisperings about what might really have occurred on that boat, especially as Anders had fled the second Lucian had reappeared.

The press repeatedly showed an athletics team photo in which a teenage Lucian stood shoulder to shoulder with a young King Niko of Piri-nu—Prince back then. Right before that accident the two men had spent several years at boarding school together. And that was why Lucian had somehow made it to Piri-nu.

There were hints that his physical recovery had taken a long time. He'd remained on Piri-nu incognito as King Niko's head of security. He'd rarely been captured on film but they'd found a few photos with him in the background—those aviator sunglasses, that muscular body. He was much tougher-looking than the charming teen he'd been in that earlier portrait.

But Lucian's fight for public approval was well and truly won, even though he'd been away for so long. In part it was because of the underlying concerns that people had about Anders. More and more horrible stories had emerged about the man.

The coverage on Zara was mixed. 'Sources' from the castle at home had asserted that Princess Zara was perfectly well and taking time for herself. Some commentators cast her as naive. Others as cold. Others still questioned how she could not have known about her fiancé's unsavoury reputation. But most were too consumed with raking through Lucian's missing years and with assessing him now.

As the days slipped by she stayed in the private wing, chatting to the same two servants who'd appeared the day after the wedding-that-wasn't. One was a man from Piri-nu who she suspected was also a soldier. The other was the man Victor, who Lucian had mentioned. He was older and had come out of retirement to serve Lucian. He was particularly attentive and had kindly asked for all her preferences. It was the first time anyone had done so and she hadn't quite known how to answer.

After that first night she'd slept deeply—still in the room that had once been his. She hadn't yet contacted her family, but she probably should soon. She should also probably move soon.

But here, for the first time, she had no need to please anyone. In this small wing she was absolutely free to be herself and figure her future out. Even if she was going to need a little more help to make it to the next stage, it was still better.

In the early evening on her fourth night of such freedom she sat in the small dining room reading more rubbish headlines on the tablet they'd provided for her while Victor placed a vast array of silver dishes on the table. There was no way she was going to be able to eat everything he was putting out for her.

That was when Lucian walked in. She ignored the thud of her heart and tried not to stare. She failed. He still looked tired. He looked leaner too—that square jaw sharper. While she'd got rest, he was seemingly still in the trenches.

'You're still here, I see.' He took off the aviator sunglasses that he so often wore and sat opposite her.

'Nowhere else I'd rather be.' She smiled at him breezily. 'The rest of the world feels sorry for me, whereas you don't actually care, and honestly that's better.'

'What makes you think I don't care?' He shot her an oblique look. 'Surely if I didn't care I would have thrown you out of the palace while you were still stuck in your wedding dress. And why do you read the rubbish if it bothers you?'

'I wasn't. I was checking the classifieds for jobs.'

'Anything appealing?'

'Sadly, there's not a lot of demand for ill-educated virgins who don't know how to turn a washing machine on.'

'And who are incapable of unbuttoning their own dresses,' he added helpfully.

'I was stitched into it, as well you know.'

'Yes. I remember.' He grinned.

She blinked at him. Then blushed.

'Is something wrong?' he asked after a moment of screaming silence.

That wariness returned and she didn't want that—so she was forced to be honest.

'You smiled.' She served herself from the dishes so she wouldn't have to look at him as she admitted that.

'And my smile rendered you speechless?'

'Only momentarily, and only because it's quite rare.' She took a large bite of food to stop herself saying anything more stupid, but the ensuing silence was even worse.

Especially as he now sat so still, apparently contemplating the vast selection of food instead of using it as a displacement activity like she was.

'They're calling it the bloodless restoration—' she tried to chat positively '—that your accession has been amazingly swift and stable.'

He nodded but that gorgeous smile still didn't return. If anything, he looked more wary.

'You're not happy about that?' she asked.

The people were still shouting his name, yet he couldn't seem to accept the adoration and accolades. Nor could he seem to decide what to eat.

'Things can change quickly,' he said before nodding to her tablet again. 'So if there are no advertised jobs that are suitable, what are your options?'

'I could work for you. Taste your food, perhaps? Make sure it isn't poisoned.'

His eyes widened. 'Pardon?'

She suddenly realised how terrible the suggestion might sound, given his past.

'It's just…' She blushed. 'You seem reluctant to eat. But I can assure you it's good. Delicious, actually.'

'I know.' He pointed towards the lamb dish. 'This was my mother's favourite. I've not eaten it in a long while.'

She stared at him in consternation. 'I'm sorry. I had no idea. Victor asked what I'd like and I wasn't sure so I asked him to prepare whatever was the usual back when you were younger…'

He still didn't answer. Still didn't move.

'I have to admit I didn't expect it to be five courses.' She offered an apologetic smile. 'I guess you were a hungry teen.'

He finally huffed a little laugh.

'I haven't felt this hungry in weeks,' she added, distracting herself from her own stupid ramblings by simply rambling more. 'I think I was anxious about the wedding.'

'Not starving yourself to fit into that dress?'

'Gosh, no. I just felt sick most of the time.'

'Not pregnant?'

'Not possible. Virgin, remember?'

His scarred eyebrow lifted. 'Stranger things have happened.'

She shot him an amazed look. 'Like once, in the Bible.'

He laughed properly this time. She stared at him, perplexed because she had the feeling he was thinking of something very specific and she couldn't fathom what. But it didn't matter because he was slowly warming up and it was a stunning revelation.

'You act like this cool customer but you're actually full drama, you know that?' She inclined her head. 'That entrance in the cathedral couldn't have been more dramatic. Especially the bare-chested bit.'

He speared her with his ice-blue gaze. 'You liked that bit?'

Now her blush engulfed every inch of her skin. 'They keep replaying it on the television, so I don't think I'm the only one who enjoyed that.'

'Seeing my scars?'

'There aren't that many scars. It was more your muscles that I found fascinating.'

He stared at her, his jaw dropping.

'I've decided that not only am I going to be selfish, I'm going to be *honest*,' she said, even as she fought her way through another atrocious blush. 'Speak freely. Let it be known what my thoughts are. No more trying to stay silent and perform prettily like a perfect princess.'

He pressed his lips together, but she saw them twitch.

'So, yes, you've got an amazing body,' she declared defiantly—her mouth running away with her again before her brain thought better. 'You didn't just recover your physical fitness. You maxed out. You're like *built*.'

'If this is yet another attempt to seduce me—'

'For the final time, I do *not* want to marry you,' she replied hotly. 'Or anyone, actually. I'm done with that.' The more honest she was, the easier it became. 'But I like looking at you. Feel free to strut about in not very much as often as you like.'

'You seem to think I'm here to serve your every request.' He laughed again. 'Thank you for giving me permission to do as I like in my own palace. Sadly for you, however, it is too cold.'

She giggled and lifted her fork in acknowledgement that he'd just won that round.

'This is really delicious,' she said. 'I can see why it was your mother's favourite.'

Unable to stop herself, she prattled on, half hoping she might make him smile some more. But while she yapped, he ate—lots—and that pleased her more than anything. He relaxed so much he even sprawled back in the seat.

'We don't dine together at home,' she informed him. 'I read. Dinner is often just a sandwich. So all this...' She gestured to the laden dishes. 'Amazing. Only now I've gorged myself to the point of discomfort. I believe it's known as emotional eating. Feeding the void inside.'

'Void?' he echoed drily.

'The lack of love from my family. The lack of purpose in my life.' Mock dolefully, she helped herself to another slice of the rich caramel apple tart just because she could. 'This gives me sweet courage. I'm not afraid of you. Or your silence.'

'And yet it seems you can't stand silence yourself. You have a need to fill it. Incessantly.'

'You mean I'm annoying?'

'No. I mean you're talkative.' His lips twitched again.

'I'll have you know it's hard work maintaining a conversation all by oneself,' she said with spirit. 'You're the one who joined me for dinner. If you wanted to eat in silence you should have taken a tray to your room.'

He sipped his wine and leaned back even more, that elusive smile playing at the corners of his mouth. 'You're saying I'm an impolite host?'

'I'm saying you're impenetrable. Fortress King Lucian.' For a moment she thought she'd gone too far. 'You're probably tired though, to be fair. Got a lot on your mind.'

'Oh, no, only a little on my mind,' he countered drily. 'So please, if you wish to converse, let us converse. What would you like to discuss?'

She met his gaze, all but dying of curiosity about so many *intimate* things. Utterly inappropriate things— like why was he as sexually inexperienced as she?

'Can you not think of anything?' he pressed when she didn't immediately reply. 'When you've been such a chatterbox until now?'

Still she could only think of intimate things. Hot things. And now her face was even hotter.

'Are you bored and lonely?' His smile was positively evil. 'Perhaps it's time for you to move on to your next phase in life. *Away* from the palace.'

'I *can* be quiet,' she declared, hardly about to concede defeat. She still had nowhere to go and nothing to get there with. 'I just need a good book.'

He blinked then a wide smile spread over his face. 'Then for heaven's sake let us find you one.' He pushed back from the table. 'Come on.'

'Now? Where?' She had to skip every few steps to keep up with him as he strode through the wing. 'What are we doing?' she puffed. 'A HIIT workout to burn off the caramel apple calories?'

He shot her an amused glance but checked the length of his strides. Finally, he opened a door and gave his customary security search look inside before standing back for her to enter.

'Oh, wow.' Zara gaped.

'You've not been in here already?' he asked.

'Of course not. I'd need a GPS system to find this and I'm not going to wander about as if I own the place.'

'But I said you have the freedom of the palace.'

'Yes, but—'

'Have you been to the indoor pool? The games room? Any of the other drawing rooms?' He looked displeased. 'Or have you just been sitting in your room marinating in the embarrassment of being jilted in front of millions?'

She gasped.

'Or perhaps watching the replays of me half-naked in the cathedral?'

He added that last so expressionlessly it was a full second before his words sank in.

'Did you just crack a joke?' Astounded, she shot him wide side-eye. 'Are you *teasing* me?'

His smile flashed. 'You do it to me all the time.'

She couldn't help laughing. 'Yes, but *that* was too far.'

'Well, you're hardly subtle sometimes.' He shrugged and walked into the library.

It didn't look as if anyone had been in here in ages. There were mountains of boxes all over the place that seemed to have been sent from publishers. They hadn't even been opened. But Zara was still catching her breath from his good humour explosion.

He studied the labels, his expression turning sombre. 'My mother had a standing order from several publishers. She liked to read the latest releases. Every quarter she would cull the collection and donate the books to various places. It looks like the books have still arrived, only to mount up over all these years. It desperately needs sorting.' He glanced at her. 'Would you do it?'

'Are you asking me to sift through all these books and decide which to keep and which to donate?'

'Yes.'

'But what would be the criteria for choosing which stay and which go?'

'Your personal preference,' he said negligently. 'I'll read anything.'

'Obviously that won't be a problem for me.'

'I didn't think it would.' He smiled again.

She hesitated, realising the truth. 'Are you just find-

ing something for me to do for a few days? Busy work
that isn't really important?'

It was awful to be so pathetic that she needed a
pity project.

'Books are very important,' he said gently. 'They
can save people from all sorts of things.'

So, yes, he was simply finding her some work, but
she also knew he wasn't entirely teasing. He meant that
last. Her curiosity mushroomed.

'Did a book save you?'

'Audio books certainly helped me rebuild my concentration and helped distract me through tough times.
I'd like others to enjoy the books that we don't need
here. They shouldn't be in boxes not being read by
anyone.'

It was the smallest personal detail and she wanted
to know much more. But he stepped back to the doorway and she instinctively moved with him.

'I truly would appreciate your assistance in dealing
with this,' he said.

'I didn't think you liked to accept assistance from
anyone.'

'In this instance I'm willing to make an exception.'

On the surface he seemed as cool as ever but something in his eyes compelled her closer. He stood so
still—half in shadow, half out of the doorway, his back
to the hinge. She realised he was ready to escape if he
needed to. He was constantly alert to his surroundings
yet he was also attentive to her and she just couldn't
drag her gaze from him.

'Then thank you,' she muttered. 'I'd like to help.'

She could do this—quite well, she thought. And
she wanted to, for herself and for him. But now nei-

ther of them moved and she realised he was staring at her mouth and she could almost *feel* it...

'Actually, there is one more thing you can do for me,' he said slowly.

'Yes?'

'Have dinner with me each night while you're here.'

She almost fell over.

'I won't disturb you with my incessant chatter?'

'Disturb?' His unscarred eyebrow quirked up. 'No. You're a good distraction.'

So she was his light relief? Her senses sharpened. She'd achieved what she'd set out to do. Only now she wanted more.

'And I realise I need to brush up on my *manners*,' he added.

'By practising on me?' Something deep inside melted and tightened at the same time. She'd told him off for his manners in the cathedral. It had been a tiny moment but he clearly remembered it. He clearly was needling her about it now, under the guise of fake politeness. His ice-blue eyes were almost dancing and she couldn't possibly refuse him.

'Of course I would be delighted to dine with you each evening,' she replied primly. 'I'm so glad to have found a small way in which I can repay your generosity. I promise I'll do my very best to distract you, Your Highness.'

'Your very best?' He seemed to consider it and find it lacking. 'What if I wanted you to do your very *worst*?'

That frisson between them shimmered.

'That wouldn't be good manners, though, would it?' she breathed.

'I thought you were done trying to be a perfect princess.'

CHAPTER SEVEN

LUCIAN'S INSISTENCE THAT she dine with him each night was a rare moment of frippery that he shouldn't have indulged in. Since when did he want companionship at meal times or any other? But he was curious about her—she was a puzzle he didn't need yet couldn't seem to put down.

Dressed in the same long black skirt and black turtleneck, she'd become an elusive shadow about the place. He'd heard her chattering to Victor from down the corridor earlier today and had felt oddly as if he were missing out on something. And as she'd demanded sanctuary from him, he reasoned dinner wasn't too much of a price for her to pay. Plus it was a complete change of pace in his otherwise incessant schedule of high-level meetings and decision-making. It was meaningless and unimportant. And he did want to spare her from being hounded by the press and whatever else she was avoiding while she sorted herself out. A couple of days more would do no harm.

Yet she shot him such a contrary look when he walked into the dining room the next night that he had to bite the inside of his cheek to stop his smile. His feelings on seeing her were equally mixed. He could just hide it better.

'Distract me, Princess.' He took the chair opposite hers. The one that afforded him a view of the door and windows. Though aside from the usual initial room scan he focused on neither. He gazed directly at her.

'Are we not here to brush up on your manners?' she enquired.

'Not tonight.'

He'd been staving off a dull headache all day, having to exert too much patience and concentration. But just looking at her restored some energy. That black outfit hid what he knew were sweet curves. Her blonde hair was in a low ponytail and she wore no make-up so her cheeks flushed. Every time she smiled her eyes sparkled. Every time she challenged him she seemed to glow. He just wanted a few moments by her fire. Yes, he was weak, but it was only dinner. Just the smallest respite.

She cocked her head. 'Shall I tell you about the miseries of my life for your entertainment?'

He sank more comfortably into his seat and drawled, 'Go on then.'

'You were witness to number one, of course.'

'I've been relegated to witness now? Not chief instigator of the wedding jilting?'

She shot him another sharp look. 'No, that was all Anders.'

'What's number two?' he prompted.

Her lips pursed. 'Are you going to respond in kind?'

'You're here as *my* entertainment. Not the other way round.'

'So I'm now your court jester.'

'If you like.' He succumbed to a devilish urge. 'I feel like you'd prefer that option to courtesan...'

'I think I'd make a marvellous courtesan if it weren't for my frigidity.'

He shrugged. 'You could always fake it.'

'True.' She suddenly sparkled and leaned a little closer. 'After all. You wouldn't know any better either.'

He slowly smiled. 'Intrigued by that fact, aren't you?'

'Surprised,' she corrected. 'There must have been the opportunity...'

'I've been very busy.' But she was right. There'd been opportunity both before the accident and after in Piri-nu all these years. But he'd not taken up the chances entirely before and he'd been determined to be duty-focused since.

'For all that time?' She shook her head. 'All work and no play...'

Made him better at his job. And he needed to be better still. But for this one moment he couldn't resist. 'Why are we talking about me?'

She pulled a face. 'You enjoy teasing me.'

Yes. He'd discovered a keen pleasure in teasing Princess Zara. She was ridiculously talkative. She didn't seem to consider what might pop out of her mouth— as if this environment were completely safe. It wasn't entirely. His inner predator itched to devour her, but he ruthlessly suppressed that part. But he let himself enjoy her artless chatter as she sampled the array of dishes the palace cooks prepared. He enjoyed watching her eat and, better still, watching her laugh. It could only be a brief interlude before going back to work. Yet he lingered over dinner. So did she.

On his way to dinner the next night his private phone rang. As only one person had the number, he answered it immediately. 'Niko?'

'You've caused quite the furore my friend.'

'Apologies if it has meant more problems or media intrusion than usual for you.'

'Oh, I can handle all that. The question is, can you?' Niko paused. 'It's been a while since you've fronted the crowds. Is there anything I can do to help?'

'I have it in hand for now, though it might be good if you visited soon to help reassure the rest of the world that we've not descended into lawless anarchy.'

'Name the date and I'll be there,' Niko immediately promised. 'What's happened to the bride? She seems to have vanished.'

Lucian hesitated. His loyalty to Niko was strong but he'd made a promise to Zara this time. 'I believe she's taking refuge while the interest rages on.'

'And Anders?'

'Won't survive long in the wild. We'll pick him up soon.' Several women had come forward, prepared to press charges against him. Anders would face justice the moment he surfaced. Lucian was confident that wouldn't be long now. 'Garth is chastened and the prosecutors are putting together the case.'

'Good,' Niko said grimly. 'Stay in touch.'

'Of course.'

Zara was already in the dining room. Preoccupied with Niko's questions, he took his seat silently and barely noticed the numerous dishes. A few minutes passed before he realised she was sitting perfectly still and staring at him.

'What?' he asked.

'Are you going to take your sunglasses off? Maybe say hello?'

He'd forgotten he was still wearing them. He took them off and shot her a deliberately broad smile. 'Better?'

She blushed and helped herself to something from a silver dish.

'The sun on the water in Piri-nu is very bright, just as it is on the snow in our mountains here. My eyes are very pale,' he found himself explaining.

She nodded. 'Was your sight damaged in the accident?'

'Fortunately not. But there wasn't good medical care in the immediate aftermath and I declined plastic surgery subsequently. I don't want to pretend that it never happened.' He ran his fingertip across the raised scar as he saw her frown. 'You think I'm wrong about that?'

'No, I don't think we can forget the events that have shaped us. At the same time, there's something to be said for healing the best you can so you can move forward and not live a life that's too impaired by something that could actually be sorted if you wanted it to be.'

She was right up to a point, but this was different. He needed to see this in the mirror every morning—to focus.

'Physical reminders matter.'

'Maybe. I guess everyone has scars, whether they're visible or not.' She looked at him. 'My skin reveals secrets without my consent. I can go all blotchy just by thinking something stupid. It's a real skill.'

'You're sensitive, that's not a bad thing.' She was human—vulnerable. 'Does anything help?'

'Avoidance of any sort of mortifying situation.'

She shouldn't be avoiding anything. She'd been hidden in a castle in her own country and she was choosing to hide again now. She should have far greater freedom.

Instead, she had another enormous dinner, tucked away in a corner of the palace, secretly keeping him company.

'This is just delicious,' she declared happily as she had yet another slice of caramel apple tart. It amused him that she liked it almost as much as he did. 'Why do I still feel like I haven't eaten in weeks?'

He had no idea, only that for him it was the same.

'I struggle to remember this isn't the last time I'll ever have this. But that I'm home. For good,' he growled. 'It's ridiculous.'

She smiled at him a little sadly. 'It'll sink in eventually, I guess.'

He didn't want her pity, he wanted distraction. That was all. 'Talk to me, Princess.'

She sighed. 'I'm not sure I have the energy for the monologue tonight.'

'It's been a challenging day?'

'Actually, I've made great progress on all your books.' Shy pride briefly illuminated her eyes before dimming. 'But I've been going round in circles about the future.'

His stomach tightened. Had she decided what she wanted to do? Was she leaving already?

'Oh?'

Zara desperately needed a more detailed plan. Instead, she was the failure her sisters had predicted she'd be when they'd patronisingly encouraged her to remain in the country and care for their parents because that was what she was 'good at'—the implication being that there wasn't anything else she could handle.

But they hadn't realised she'd done more than simply bring them trays of tea and cake. She'd ended up running the castle, being the one to deal with the contractors and suppliers in the never-ending quest to stop it falling down. So surely she could figure out her future, it couldn't be anywhere near as complex as repairing the collapsed north wing had been.

'Maybe being stuck in the library all day isn't ideal,' he said. 'Some physical activity might help your mood.'

She felt that frisson scrape her nerves. 'Does it help yours?' she asked softly.

'Often and absolutely,' he answered with a glint in his eyes. 'Not just my mood but my entire wellbeing.'

'Gosh,' she marvelled. 'So what physical activity is your favourite?'

He almost smiled. He knew, didn't he, that she was endlessly curious about him, that she was even more intrigued by that elusive smile and the brief flashes of the charming young prince he'd once been. But he didn't pick up on the less than subtle sensual turn their conversation was taking.

'I like building things,' he said, leaning back and watching her expression with an amused one of his own. 'I worked on a building for Niko for a long time.'

Yes, she'd read that in his time on Piri-nu he'd lived for the best part of two years on King Niko's private island. 'Was this the holiday home?'

'It was badly damaged in a cyclone. Took a lot of

time to rebuild, actually.' He nodded. 'It was a way of maintaining my physical fitness.'

Yes, Lucian had rebuilt himself. And then the house. And now his monarchy.

'Sadly, you don't seem to have a house for me to literally rebuild, so what alternative physical activity would you suggest?' she enquired a little too innocently.

His mouth twitched. 'Given you're concerned about the sensitivity of your skin, perhaps something indoors might be best.'

'Indoors, you think?'

He inhaled deeply. 'Tell me about the situation in Dolrovia.'

She smiled as he changed topic. 'Do you want the diplomatic, docile Princess's response or my actual opinion?'

He did smile then. 'You choose.'

'We're a small nation, dependent on good trade ties with those nearest and there isn't a need for its old Royal family any more. There hasn't been for a long time. But my father can't accept the reality that the duty he was born for doesn't exist any more. They've become something of an embarrassment with their belief in their grandeur. Especially for my more modern older sisters.'

'And for you?' he said. 'You're unusually reticent about your reasons for wanting to escape, Zara.'

'Honestly, it doesn't seem right to moan about my life, given what you've endured. I'm going to sound pathetic.'

'Shall I tell you what I know already? I know your

parents were older when they had you. You were very much a 'late lamb' who—'

'Was a disappointment because I wasn't a boy.'

'So you weren't an indulged baby?'

'There was nothing to indulge me with.'

'Not even attention?' He watched her curiously.

Definitely not that. Zara sighed—if he really wanted to know, she would tell him. She was the distraction, after all.

'Despite our family finances heading into decline, my parents kept spending as if every cent earned in Dolrovia was theirs by divine right. Maximum consumption. The public weren't crazy about it and parliament hit them with their first ever tax bill. My older sisters were already educated and had built their lives. Mia works in an art gallery and is engaged, while Ana's a successful academic at the university—both of which are considered acceptable roles. They like their life in the city and it doesn't matter that our titles will die with us. Neither of them wants to deal with our stuck-in-the-last-century parents. But I was young when they were deposed and my parents couldn't afford the fees to send me to the same elite school. My parents wouldn't let me go to the local one because that would look even more *shameful* and common.'

'Hence the nineteenth-century governess business.'

'Exactly.' She shot him a small smile. 'That was just one way they tried to hide the true state of our affairs. So, while theoretically I'm still a princess, there's no power, no perks, no privileges. My duty is to my parents and that's okay, but they allow me no self-determination. They seemed to think I'd always be there

and to the rest of the world I've just been kind of…
forgotten about.'

'What do you do all day in this prison?'

'I try to accommodate the demands of an old king
who still can't grasp he has no power.' She paused and
lifted her chin. 'I actually have taken on a lot of the
admin of running the castle, and some of that is okay,
but the problem is there's no choice and no chance
for anything different. That's what I'm angry about. I
don't expect things to be handed to me. I *want* to work
but my parents view paid work as beneath Royal life.
My sister Ana gets away with her career only because
she's literally a genius and so has actually brought us
a sort of prestige, and Mia is so stunning she's really
the 'art' in the gallery. I can't even do charitable work
because apparently that would require me to have a
designer wardrobe that they can't afford. Not to mention the fact that I lack the right social skills because
I get too awkward and babble and the nerves have to
be covered up.' But she'd never been given the experience to overcome them. She'd done what she could in
the castle—taking over the official correspondence as
well. Her parents weren't even aware she did all that—
a small fact always made her smile, somewhat sadly.

'The total control isn't protective, it's not because
they care about *me,* but more how our circumstances
look. I'm not as pretty as Mia, not as smart as Ana, and
neither of *them* are interested in helping me because
it's convenient that I remain in the country bearing
the burden of our parents' demands and they can just
live their lives…' She sighed. 'While I was younger I
guess that made sense. But they barely know me now,
yet they've always said over and over that they know

how happy I am in the country, how I would hate to have to work in the city, that I don't understand what having to work in the real world is like…'

She looked at his deepening frown. 'And maybe I don't understand all that, but only because I've never been given the chance to try and they don't stop to listen. I need to get on with my own life and not be dependent upon the little that's left. It's not like here, where the Royal family still carries such importance.'

'So that's why you sought importance with Anders?'

She shook her head. It wasn't about importance as such. 'I just don't want to waste my life and I don't want to be lonely. And I have been.' She shrugged. 'I wanted to be what my family needed me to be. I wanted to please them. I thought the engagement would do that…'

'And it did?'

'First time my mother actually gushed over me.' She wrinkled her nose. 'But you know I don't feel the need to please them any more.'

'Fair enough,' he said and drew in a deep breath. 'So now what?'

Frankly, her plan was pretty nebulous and definitely required some assistance. Something she was instinctively still wary of asking him for.

'I'm slowly working that out…'

His hard expression eased. 'I suppose I can handle your presence a little while longer.'

'I'm sorry. I've been pretty useless 'til now.'

'I disagree, I've seen those boxes of books you've sorted already. I think you're clever and curious. I definitely think you're courageous. And I think you care about a lot of things. You'll get there.'

The decisions she'd made so far hadn't exactly been

brilliant but his confidence in her was kind. Except she didn't really want his *kindness* now either.

'Well,' She looked at the table, embarrassed by her own docility for all these years. 'The best decision I've made today was asking for the caramel apple tart again, right?'

The next night Lucian frowned when he got to the dining room. The dinner dishes were in place but Zara was nowhere to be seen. He listened but couldn't hear her footsteps or chatter. Two minutes later he paused in the open doorway of the library and checked it over. Boxes of books were now neatly stacked, labelled and sorted. Yeah, not useless at all, Zara had cleared the large table and was now sitting at it in her long-sleeved black turtleneck and that long black skirt, with her long blonde hair tumbling down her back. Her face was still pale but vitality sparkled in her blue eyes as she concentrated on whatever she was writing. He couldn't resist walking in, closing the door behind him.

'You are late and I am hungry. You know you don't have to spend every waking moment sorting this, it doesn't matter if you don't ever finish it before—' He broke off. He didn't like to think of her leaving.

'I've actually thought of something else I could do for you,' she said quietly.

His body leapt to attention.

'I wondered if I could help with the palace correspondence.'

Not *quite* where his mind had gone, but she had such nervousness in her blue eyes, he needed to pay attention to her. She was sweetly earnest.

'Have you seen all the mail filling up the purple stateroom?' she added.

Uh, no. He hadn't been in that stateroom in years. She stood and picked up a box from behind her and lifted it onto the table. It wasn't full of books but cards, letters, posters, paintings even. Lucian's chest tightened. He'd been stalling on engaging directly with the public. He'd needed to focus on the politicians first.

'I've been watching the constant deliveries into the courtyard from the library window. I asked them to bring me a selection.' She looked awkward. 'I hope you don't mind.'

'Mind you reading correspondence meant for me?' He tried to tease but his voice was suddenly rusty.

'I thought I might be able to help you answer some.'

He stared, surprised she'd even want to.

'I do sort of know how palaces are run,' she muttered quickly. 'Especially when there are limitations on staff, and your staff are really busy right now.'

He glanced down at the table and saw she'd written screeds in strong, clear script.

'I draft my father's letters,' she added. 'So I've written some responses to the sorts of letters you've been getting. A skeleton response is easy to tweak and personalise for each. They should get a reply, given they've taken the time to write to you.'

She was right. He quickly skimmed what she'd written. It was good.

'Isn't your father missing you doing this for him now?'

Colour washed over her skin and an intriguingly cheeky smile lit up her face. 'He doesn't know I do it. When I was younger the communications team was in the room next to my schoolroom. It was the most fun room in the place. My governess realised I liked reading and writing and figured I could be left in there while she went and flirted with one of locals in the village. As we lost more and more staff, I took on more and more—not just correspondence with the public, but the contractors and general management of the castle.'

Judging from what she'd written here, she was good at it.

'So you *do* work,' he said. 'It's just that it's unpaid and unrecognised. Wouldn't your father appreciate this if he knew?'

She shook her head. 'I'm scared he would stop me.'

Well, the last thing Lucian wanted was to stop her doing something she wanted, but at the same time *he* wasn't going to take advantage of her. 'If you do this, I'll pay you.'

She frowned.

'You will not be a slave for me, Zara.'

'Well, I don't want you to be my *boss*.' She looked grumpy. 'You're helping me, I'm helping you. That's all. I'm giving you some of my time to repay your hospitality, just like how you helped repay Niko with your time and skills.' Her eyes sparkled. 'Have you read *any* of these letters?'

'Obviously I've not yet had time.'

But he didn't really *want* to. He'd been resisting this more intimate, direct contact with his people. He knew he needed to see them and speak directly to them but he couldn't quite face it yet. His mother had been a wonderful Queen. Selfless and loyal, she'd been deeply loved by everyone. Lucian wanted to honour her legacy and live up to the example she'd set. But he wasn't there yet. It was going to take him time to get anywhere near her level—that undivided attention for the next decade.

Zara lifted a page from a neat pile. 'Read this one.'

Reluctantly, he took the paper she held out for him. It was handwritten and he frowned in an effort to decipher the spidery writing. It was from an elderly resident of Monrayne who remembered not just his mother and father, but his grandfather too. It included everything he'd feared. It gushed with pleasure at his return, detailing hope and pride in his reign—remembrances of the greatness of his mother and her father. He could never live up to the ideal this man wanted.

Because he was a fraud. He hadn't been anywhere near a good enough son to his mother. He'd not listened closely enough, he'd mulishly wanted his own time, he'd let her down so completely—futility flooded him, pushing him back into that angry corner where memories made mincemeat of his soul.

Someone touched his arm. He instantly spun, instinctively grabbing the assailant and neutralising the threat.

'Lucian?'

His pulse thundered. Zara was a breath from him. Her blue eyes flared wide. Her wrist was in his hand.

'I didn't mean to startle you,' she said.

He'd been so lost in his own quagmire of bitterness he'd not been aware how close she'd got. Yet he didn't release her. Instead, he drew her closer still.

'I said your name like three times,' she added a touch defensively.

He breathed out harshly. He was *always* fully attentive to his surroundings. To any possible threat. But somehow she'd literally sneaked under his guard.

'You're probably used to a different name,' she said, breaking the searing silence.

Zara was the only name in his head right now. It was Zara's fault. Zara who distracted him in so *many* ways.

'Pax…?'

So she'd been paying attention to the information the media had been ruthlessly excavating about him. *Pax* was the name he'd used in all his time away—when there'd been no title, no expectation, only anonymity. Where—in theory—he could do what he wanted. *Selfishly.* Which was his true self after all—like the teen who'd taken off on holiday instead of taking on work for his mother. And he'd reverted to type—the urge within him now was nothing but selfish. The hunger that had driven him to this room slipped its disguise. It wasn't *dinner* he wanted to have with her.

'Don't call me that,' he growled, tightening his grip on her.

She'd been his nemesis's fiancée. A fact he absolutely and irrationally *loathed,* even though he knew it had been nothing for her other than a means of escape. She hadn't known she'd have been going from frying pan to fire. But now she'd landed in an infinitely hotter, more dangerous hell. With him.

'I apologise, Your Highness.'

But she didn't look sorry. Her eyes glinted with something more fiery. His title was the *last* thing he wanted to be reminded of.

'Don't call me that either,' he snapped.

'Then what?'

Forbidden desire roared—not just deafening him but swamping his reason. The only thing he could do was silence her taunting mouth with his own. He smashed his lips onto hers. Instantly the provocation increased threefold. Because she melted against him, her softness entirely his to enjoy. He swept inside her sweet mouth—tasting the heat of her, revelling in the touch he'd been aching to feel for ever. The hunger that hadn't been assuaged in days was now ravenous and there was no getting close enough, no number of kisses that could possibly satisfy him. But that didn't stop him trying. He released her wrist and wrapped his arms around her. Clamping her to him, he plundered her soft lips and hot mouth with increasing greed.

Zara gripped his shirt, desperate to keep him close as desire was unleashed. She burned with an unfettered need to reach him. She rose on tiptoe, deepening the kisses, seeking to push closer still. His growl of hunger, of pleasure, of desire made her entire body tremble.

Only just as swiftly as it had ignited, it ended. With another guttural growl he sharply pulled away. She would have stumbled had he not kept that firm grip on her waist. But, instead of holding her close, he kept her literally at his arm's length now and she couldn't catch her breath.

'Don't tell me you're speechless?' He finally spoke. 'Now I know how to get some peace around here.'

'Was that just a way to shut me up?' Zara panted, hurt.

Because she wanted it to be more. She wanted it to happen again. But, as she watched, wariness returned to his expression. Worse, she swore she read *regret*. His walls were rebuilding before her eyes.

'Zara—'

'You must think I'm a terrible person.' She cut

him off before he could say anything to make her feel worse.

He looked appalled. 'Why would I think that?'

Scalding-hot embarrassment crawled over every inch of her. She could prattle on about meaningless things easily enough, but talking about anything deeply personal or important was much harder. But, despite her awkward shyness, she had to explain because she refused to let him minimise what had just happened. That kiss hadn't been trivial for her.

'Because only a few days ago I was going to marry someone else and now I just want to kiss you.'

'You never wanted to kiss Anders?'

'I tried not to think about it.'

'The first time you kissed him was going to be at the wedding?'

'That was going to be the first time I kissed anyone.'

There was a long pulsing pause. She saw the heat reignite within him—his pale irises obliterated by the dark pupils.

'I don't give a damn about Anders,' he growled. 'I will not allow him to steal a minute more of my life or my mind. If you want to kiss me then you just go ahead and kiss me. You're not trapped in your castle now, Zara. You can do whatever you want.'

The heat overwhelming her was now fuelled by desire. He was testing the truth of her assertion and she wouldn't shy away from his challenge. She stepped closer as he remained frozen in place beside the large table.

He was so very still. But she had his permission. And she would use it. She had to rise right onto her tiptoes again—and even then it was a stretch—so with a trembling hand she grabbed his shirt again and tugged. For a split-second he remained like a statue. But then another groan escaped him and he bent and she pressed her mouth to his. His movement then was swift and complete. She was crushed in his arms before he spun them both and somehow she was on her back on that table and he was pinning her there as he kissed her and it was heaven.

'Zara...' He paused for just a moment and met her eyes. When he smiled he stole her breath. Which meant she had no chance of survival in this moment. Suddenly she was greedy. She tugged his shirt again, pulling him back.

'You want more?' he asked thickly.

'I want it all,' she confessed. She'd never had it—not anything like *this*.

Because this wasn't just kissing, this was touch, this was heat and light and such tormenting pleasure. The need, the delight quickened and deepened. He stroked her so cleverly, his fingers teasing her taut nipples through her top, sliding beneath the waistband of her skirt, rendering her weak and willing and hot.

She shuddered at the sheer eroticism of his touch as his fingers delved lower still. 'I thought you said you were a virgin,' she gasped.

'I am,' he muttered, pressing hot kisses up her neck before teasing her mouth again. 'But I'm not completely inexperienced. I know how to please a woman.'

Oh. He did. He really did. Zara arched, grateful that she was on the table and didn't have to take her own weight. But she was desperate for *his*. She wanted his massive, hard body pressing utterly and absolutely *into* her. But she couldn't speak now—unwilling to ever break this kiss. She spread her legs wider, letting him slide his fingers against her even more intimately, her sighs quickening as he did. She never wanted this to end. Yet the sweeping rise of her arousal was unstoppable. She moaned again and again—breathless and hot and feeling as if every cell within her was shimmering.

'Take pleasure from me, Zara,' he growled roughly.

Honestly, he gave her no choice. He kissed her ruthlessly and his fingers teased right where she was so sensitive, so wet, so deeply aching. She bucked against him, her body shuddering as he stroked her to the brink and beyond—her next sigh cut short by a harsh scream of pleasure. Spasms shook her and he pressed close, anchoring her through the ecstasy.

When she finally opened her eyes she was too dazed to interpret the depths in his, but she felt the gentleness with which he readjusted her clothes and released her from that intimate hold. She'd never experienced anything like it and she was still too stunned to speak. But he wasn't.

'Zara, I'm so sorry. That shouldn't have happened,' he said huskily. 'I showed an unforgivable lack of self-control.'

CHAPTER EIGHT

LUCIAN HAD NO idea *how* he'd walked away. Only that it had been imperative he had before he'd lost all control and taken exactly what he wanted with no thought to the consequences. He'd not slept. He'd worked through—determined to focus on his work. These were long days and the level of concentration required in the meetings was intense. What she'd shown him last night—one letter of thousands—should have helped him stay on track. Instead, he'd been overwhelmed by a temptation unlike any other. For years he'd avoided emotional entanglements, not wanting to risk exposure or identification, and because he'd been determined to maintain his single-minded focus on rebuilding his health and resources in readiness for his revenge and restoration. But these last two had come so shockingly swiftly now.

Was this bone-deep need for her simply the result of such long self-denial? An outlet for the stress of the situation? A new fixation to fill the void? The answer mattered little because the total loss of control just couldn't happen again. For *her* sake more than his. He couldn't trifle with her. She didn't deserve to be messed around by another Monrayne Royal. She'd been publicly crushed and her future was uncertain. That was enough. And he needed to put his country first for a long, long time—the decade he'd promised. He had no room for anything more with anyone. So he needed to stop this now.

All day he resisted the urge to seek her out. To say sorry again. To kiss her again. But he walked more quickly than usual to the dining room that next night. Then he saw the determinedly proud tilt to her chin.

'*Manners*,' she said pointedly the moment he took the seat opposite hers. 'Let's discuss them.'

'Manners in what setting?' he answered with more calm than he was feeling.

'The bedroom.' Her cheeks were scarlet and the pink blotches extended down to her neck.

She really wanted to go there right away? Of course she did. This sweet princess could be astoundingly brave. And blunt. Well, so could he.

'I don't recall us making it to a bedroom, Zara.' His muscles rippled with the recollection of her on that table, her soft body pressed beneath his as he'd cupped her hot, slick core.

'Sexual relations then, you know what I mean.'

'Did I not please you?' he asked quietly.

She swallowed. 'The problem is more that *I* didn't please you.' Her voice was low and husky.

His entire body tensed as he was engulfed by a sexual ache so strong he had to grit his teeth.

'It pleased me to please you.'

There was another moment where he just knew she was summoning her strength too.

'Was that really enough for you?' she asked.

He couldn't answer.

'You didn't have to do anything at all if you didn't really want to,' she said resentfully.

His hold began to slip. Her guilelessness and her dauntlessness were both unique and irresistible. 'I was the one who started it, remember?'

'And then challenged me to take more if I wanted.'

Yes. He'd selfishly sought her attentions—greedily aching to know she desired him the way he did her, and then he'd lost himself, desperate to discover her and yes, to please her. But he lost control with no one, and she threatened that rule so completely with her all-in softness and heat. Hell, she'd only had to look at him and she'd made his resolve evaporate. When he desperately needed to be better for his country, this self-indulgence was unacceptable.

'And then you just left,' she added.

She was right and that had been unacceptable of him too. He cursed himself inwardly. He needed to be mindful not just of his duty to his country, but of his duty of care towards her.

'It was better to walk away than to do something that couldn't be taken back,' he said tightly.

'Was that what was about to happen?'

His gut twisted. 'Zara…'

Her vitality and *honesty* challenged him. She had such courage. Maybe he needed more of the same. His hunger for her wasn't going to disappear. But maybe they could restrain it—allow a manageable, acceptable level of release. Maybe that was the only way through here. Because they *couldn't* go all in. That wasn't right for either of them. But if they compromised just a little they could at least *ease* the ache enough to survive it.

* * *

Zara furiously stared at him, trying to work him out. He'd given her such pleasure, only then apparently regretted it so intensely that he'd walked out on her. She wanted to know *why*. Why, when he'd kissed her, when he'd made her come apart in complete pleasure…why had he left so quickly?

Because for her it had been a revelation and she wanted more of it. *With* him.

'Would you walk away without taking pleasure from me again?' she asked.

She wanted to be intimate with him, but not if he wasn't going to allow her to give him that pleasure too.

His tension mounted. 'You can trust that I will not take your virginity.'

She did trust him. With all of her body. 'So you'll only go so far, is that what you're saying?'

He closed his eyes briefly. 'Yes.'

Her blood hummed. He would touch her but not take all of her. And he wouldn't give her all of him either.

'Don't you trust me?' she asked softly.

His eyes flashed open and he stared at her directly. 'I don't trust anyone. Ever.'

'You trust Niko,' she pointed out. 'He's never let you down.'

'Niko can take care of himself. I don't have to worry about him.'

'You don't have to worry about me either.' Her anger spiked.

'More importantly—' he ignored her interruption '—I won't take advantage of you.'

'I don't need you to *patronise* me.' She lifted her head proudly. 'I'm not going to be here for long, Lucian. I'm going to leave. Why can't we enjoy what's between us? It wouldn't be taking advantage. It would only be for a little—'

'Zara—'

'You're not going to break my heart—' she brazenly asked outright for what she wanted '—it's just sex.'

He shook his head but his eyes glowed. 'It wouldn't be right for us to go that far, Zara.'

'Why not?'

'You've just been jilted at the altar. Is this the best time to make that decision? And you know that if anyone found out, it would make things even more complicated for us both. Not in a good way.'

Annoyed because she could see his point but hurt by yet another rejection, she snapped back, piqued, 'Fine, maybe I'll just *please myself*, as you once so wisely suggested.'

'Really?' He suddenly shot her a tight, feral smile. 'I think you might find that that's not the same now. It won't be enough.'

'We'll see, I guess.' She shrugged even as her insides seemed to melt.

'All right,' he said silkily. 'Why don't you prove it to me?'

She stilled. 'Now?'

'Why not?' he challenged provocatively. 'Go on, Zara. You do you.'

The atmosphere crackled. It was as if she were thrown right back into that sensual crucible he'd created for her in his arms last night.

'Is that what gets you going—*watching*?' But she felt her skin flush. What he was daring was outrageous, yet she was dangerously hot. 'Can't you let yourself be touched?'

She heard his sharp intake of breath. In the next second he pushed away from the table, stalked around to her seat and pulled her out of it. The second after that she was clutching his shoulders as he bent her back and kissed her straight back to the searing edge of ecstasy. His hands were *almost* everywhere—his clever, tormenting, sweeping hands that stopped just short of where she burned most for him.

'See?' he growled fiercely. 'It's not enough. You need *my* touch. You ache for it.'

It had seemed like such a good idea to challenge him directly but now, as she writhed against him in shocking desperation, she felt utterly undone by her own desire.

'And I will touch you, Zara. I will kiss you. I can give you the satisfaction you crave,' he muttered hotly against her throat. 'But *only* up to a point. You won't suffer *harm* from me. You've suffered enough of that with Anders.'

'He never touched me,' she growled back. 'And you taking my virginity *wouldn't* harm me.'

'I will *not* hurt you, Zara,' he gritted hoarsely.

'That wouldn't happen!'

But he stilled.

Anger swamped her at the impasse. She'd been so alone, so forgotten, and she'd tried to sacrifice so much. With him—in this—she suddenly wanted *everything*. Not the few crumbs he cared to toss her way. And she could *feel* his arousal against her right now. Why was he so determined to deny them both this release?

'I'm tired of people pretending I don't exist,' she

said in frustration. 'Of ignoring my desires. My wishes have value.'

'And I will do everything *else* you wish,' he argued.

She ached as he stood so close she could feel his uneven breathing, but she didn't want to feel this emptiness. She didn't want to settle for less any more. She made herself push him back, *hard*.

'Then I want *nothing* of that from you.'

He stepped back. 'What?'

'I say no. To everything.'

Astonishment flashed in his eyes. 'All or nothing? Is that your position?'

'Yes. We either go all the way or we don't go anywhere.' She just knew she was scarlet in the face as she said that.

He stared at her and the most fascinating smile tugged at the corners of his mouth. 'I think I can make you change your mind.'

Now she was so angry she almost stomped her foot. 'You don't take me seriously?'

His gaze hardened and, impossibly, the atmosphere thickened with the fire of challenge. 'I take you extremely seriously. And I will be extremely serious in my efforts to win a compromise from you.'

Win? The arrogance angered her but the *playfulness* simply stunned her. Who *was* this man?

'Because you just have to win?' she asked huskily. 'I didn't think you would play such games.'

'Perhaps I surprise us both,' he agreed. 'But surely you must concede that *some* is better than none.'

'I thought you were all about protecting me from harm and being honourable.'

'I am.' He cupped her face. '*Neither* of us is in a position to handle a full-blown affair. I have too much work. You have too much uncertainty.'

Neither of us. That little admission soothed something deep inside, reminding her that he too was at sea. He too faced all kinds of upheavals and challenges right now.

'But perhaps we can handle a little indulgence. The slightest, smallest tryst. Just to smooth the edge off it.'

Tryst? He was trying to contain this—he wouldn't even call it an affair.

'Control is important to you,' she said slowly.

'You want control over your life too. Correct? Face it, Zara. Both of us have too much else going on to deal with anything too intense.'

She felt a little hit inside. Because he was right. But while he was offering to tease and flirt and give her unspeakable pleasure, though it was the most tempting offer of her life, she *couldn't* agree to it. She couldn't let that be enough.

'Then I think it's best that we not deal with it at all.'

'Ignore it?' He shook his head. 'That won't work.'

'Sure it will,' she said resolutely. 'That's what you excel at, Lucian.'

'What?'

'You think I can't handle you—that's why you're so honourably suggesting we keep this under "control". But I think the truth is that *you* can't handle *me*. You literally ran away from me last night.'

'Because—'

'You haven't let yourself have any fun in *years*,' she said hotly. '*I* haven't had the chance to have fun before, but *you* have. You've made it your *choice* not to indulge.'

He stared at her. Silenced. But she saw the flare in his eyes and knew she was onto something.

'What's holding you back, Lucian?' Did he not want to be vulnerable with anyone—or did he feel as if he shouldn't have pleasure for some reason?

He didn't answer. And that was an answer in itself. It came back to trust.

She leaned closer to him. 'Until you're able to talk to me, there's nothing. Until you can allow yourself to indulge in pleasure—in *all* intimacy—then there'll be none. At least not with me.' She squared her shoulders. 'Now, let me sit down. I refuse to let this delicious dinner get cold.'

There was a long moment when she really wasn't sure what he was going to do. There was a wildness in his eyes and she felt like he was either going to storm out and slam the door, or tumble her to the floor and take her here and now.

He did neither. He stepped back and took his seat at the table. But that glittering emotion in his eyes heightened every one of her senses.

Too late she remembered that Lucian Monrayne had already proven himself a patient man. And one who always ensured he got payback.

Lucian had once prided himself on patience. He'd thought he could play a long game. In this case, he was utterly wrong. He paced through the palace, burning with frustration. Wanting her to say yes to anything he asked. Like a dictator. Like a selfish, lustful jerk. What was so awful about the proposal to be together yet remain within controllable, easily definable boundaries?

'I'm going on a tour of the country,' he told her the

next night at dinner. 'I need to be seen everywhere and by everyone. It is important for security and confidence in my return.'

'How long are you going for?'

Her crestfallen expression demolished him even more.

'Why? Will you miss me?' he asked.

'I doubt I'll notice your absence, I'm far too busy.'

'Is that so?' he said drily. 'I'm only taking day trips. I'll return to the palace every night so you're still stuck with my company for dinner.'

She looked at him for a long moment. 'You're ready to spend time with your people now?'

He stiffened because no, he wasn't really. 'I need to.'

'You're a good listener, Lucian. They love you already. Listen and smile and they'll love you even more.'

He looked into her wide eyes and appreciated that she really meant that. She was too sweet.

Only she suddenly frowned. 'You won't tell anyone I'm still here?'

'It amazes me that you doubt this, Zara. Please be assured I *can* keep a secret.'

She smiled suddenly and he couldn't resist nudging her chin up and stealing a kiss. It was hardly theft though, was it—when she softened in response, when she opened to him like a flower. When she lifted her hands and touched him until he growled in pleasure. He lifted away and gazed into her dazed eyes. But then they gleamed with something else.

'Dare you to tell me one of yours,' she teased.

Yet it wasn't a tease. This was a battle. They wanted each other, yes, but he knew she was vulnerable. More than she wanted to admit. Taking her luscious offer now would be doing her a disservice. She was alone, feeling abandoned by her family and perhaps simply seeking comfort from him. He couldn't take total advantage. She deserved more than that.

He liked her more with every moment he spent with her. There'd been too many of those moments already, when Monrayne needed his full attention. He'd made that vow to serve his country. It was weak to be sidetracked so soon. It simply served to remind him he still wasn't worthy of his Crown—he was still putting personal pleasure ahead of duty.

Yet she was determined to crack him open emotionally. And while he tried to keep her at arm's length, he ended up pulling her close and silencing her with his mouth after all. He couldn't resist sparring with her—even if it were sometimes just silly double-entendres designed to make that dusky bloom appear like magic on her silky skin. She was extra delicious when she blushed.

At the end of the evening his usual cold shower no longer cut it. He went to the gym for a workout. Then to the pool. Then to the ice bath at the end of it.

He'd just immersed himself—cursing inwardly—when Zara appeared like the elusive shadow she was—haunting him even more than ever and making him forget every good intention he'd just managed to resurrect.

'What are you doing?' She halted.

She had a swimsuit in her hands. It seemed she'd taken his advice for some physical exercise seriously.

'What does it look like?' he gritted.

'Torture.' She stared in horror. 'Your extremities

will·fall off. Which would be a shame. You have nice...'
she glanced at him archly '...fingers.'

'You're worried about my fingers?'

She studied her own fingers for a second before
shooting him another coy look from beneath her lashes.
'Amongst other things, yes.'

He chuckled. 'Ice baths bring mental clarity,' he explained. 'I need to think.'

'Oh? Have you forgotten how?'

'Around you, it seems I have.'

She gaped for a split-second, then smiled. 'I will
take that as a compliment.'

He reached for a towel, hiding his reaction to her before standing up. To his immense pleasure, she didn't
step away—she couldn't. Apparently she was transfixed by his bare chest. Yeah, sometimes a man had
to play dirty—with whatever cards he held.

'You're cold,' she muttered distractedly as he
stepped nearer.

'Then help me warm up,' he breathed. 'Kiss me,
Zara.'

She did. His skin heated the second it touched hers.
But after the merest moment she shivered and pushed
back on him. Reluctantly he stepped back, meeting her
beautiful, baleful blue eyes.

'You don't play fair,' she muttered.

No. He didn't. He never really had.

Zara sat in the library, quietly trying to ignore the fact
that frustration was killing her. Lucian been away from
the palace all day—welcomed with thousands cheering
in the streets. She felt absurdly jealous of them. She

wanted that time with him—because there could only
be a little left. She had to leave soon.

So she wanted to change *his* mind because there
were already onerous limits upon them. She understood
his rationale and yes, to anyone on the outside, the two
of them tumbling into a hot-blooded affair would be
insane, given her uncertain future and the public pres-
sures he faced. But the intensity with which she wanted
him was like nothing she'd ever felt and, frankly, she
feared she'd never feel it again. No other man had ever
been as attractive to her and, sure, she'd not met many
but no man in the world was like Lucian.

And she wanted to feel as if she finally had her own
life in her own hands. That she could actually get this
one thing she actually, really wanted. That she could
be independent and strong in making choices for herself before she left here for good.

She had more of an idea now. She didn't want to ask
Lucian for financial help, given things had got complicated between them personally. It was embarrassing but she was going to have to reach out elsewhere.
She couldn't stay in Monrayne, nor could she return
to Dolrovia. So she was going to draft a letter to a distant cousin of her father to ask for a small loan and
hope she'd agree. Then she'd go to England. It would
be far enough away and big enough to give her a little
anonymity. She'd take on an unskilled job, study in
the evenings and repay the loan as soon as she could.
People did that all the world over. She could too. And
there were plenty of enormous old houses that needed
management—that was what she was good at and, honestly, she'd liked her old castle far more than her family

at times. A bubble of enthusiasm lifted her low spirits. She could definitely do that.

'Hello, Zara.' He tipped her face back and kissed her thoroughly.

She was so surprised she couldn't speak. She hadn't even heard him walk into the room.

He laughed as he pulled away. 'My manners are improving, yes?'

'You call those manners?' The man was taking liberties. 'I'm not your therapy dog who you can pet for comfort and then just ignore whenever you feel like it.'

'Ignore?' His eyebrows shot up. 'What's happened to put you in such a snit?'

'A snit?'

'Yes. A mood. Has something happened?'

'Since when do you care?'

'Wow. Okay. Won't ask again. Will just go away quietly and consume dinner alone.'

She glared at him. The last thing she wanted was for him to retreat into silence.

'Stupid article—' she opted for the least of her concerns '—from my stupid country. I am a disappointment to the entire nation now, not just my family.'

He gestured dismissively at the tablet on the table. 'Why do you *still* read them?'

'As if you don't?'

'I only do because I need to be aware of the mood, whether there are any rumblings. It's an intelligence-gathering exercise. You're out of this now, you don't need to bother.'

'But I'm the one they're judging.'

'They can't judge you when they don't even know you.'

'Doesn't stop them trying though, does it.' She

sighed. 'I went from being the princess everyone had forgotten about to a supposedly perfect bride, which we all know is an impossibility. To the poor unwanted princess who's a coward.'

'You're not a coward, you're very brave. Not to mention beautiful.'

She had no time for flattery from him. 'Yet you resist me so easily.'

'On the contrary, it is you who resists me.' He shot her a look. 'I would be on my knees between your legs right now if you gave the nod.'

Her face flamed at the image he'd just put in her head. 'I can't. Not while you don't trust me enough to believe me when I say I know what I want and I can handle it.'

He regarded her in silence and that made her resentment burn hotter. She was sleepless. But he looked exhausted. He was pushing himself too hard.

'I mean it,' she said, knowing she was provoking him and doing it anyway. 'You should see a therapist for your trust issues.'

His mouth twisted. 'You think I can trust a therapist?'

'It is a conundrum,' she acknowledged. 'But you're going to need to trust someone some time or everything you're doing is pointless.'

He stiffened. 'It's not pointless to protect my people.'

'They survived without you before. They would again. No one is indispensable.'

'You're saying I'm unnecessary?'

'I think your *personal* sacrifices are unnecessary. You've given up too much of yourself and too much of your life already.'

'And you've not wanted to make sacrifices for your country or your family?' He regarded her sardonically.

But there was more to this. More she couldn't let go.

'I think I was far more selfish than you, actually.' She narrowed her eyes as he paled at her words. 'I think you don't want to trust anyone because you don't want to be hurt.'

'You don't think my lack of trust has anything to do with the fact that my cousin…'

'Your cousin what?' she recklessly pressed. 'What really happened that day, Lucian?'

Lucian clamped his jaw shut and stared at her. The exhaustion from touring was getting to him, as was the frustration of being around her and being unable to touch her in the way he craved more and more. He'd been so looking forward to seeing her he'd just *had* to kiss her. And now—

Now she'd stilled.

And he *had* worked his issues through with a therapist, as it happened. He'd taken that chance while in Piri-nu in an effort to work out if he could truly trust what he'd seen that day. But now he was furious, and Zara was looking at him with her big blue eyes and he knew she wanted more than the scant details that he'd given to the press. She wanted to know *why*. But there was so much more to it than that one morning.

'Anders came to live with us when he was seven,' he said roughly. 'My mother had already lost my father and then her sister and her husband died in a plane crash. As Anders was their only child, of course she opened up the palace to him. My mother was generous.' He took in a breath, remembering his mother's hurt and hating it. 'Garth came too. He's Anders's uncle. He always seemed reliable and willing to assist. My mother trusted him. I'd just gone to boarding school abroad so I saw Anders only in the holidays. Frankly, I wasn't as patient as I could have been. I thought he was always a bit spoiled. Of course I was equally spoiled, but I was just too arrogant to see it.'

'So you weren't close?'

'Not as close as we could have been.' If Lucian had made more effort, maybe things might have turned out differently—that was on him too. 'My mother wanted me to mentor him but I wasn't that good at it. I wasn't…'

'But you took him on that holiday with you,' Zara prompted. 'You took him diving.'

Only because he'd been made to.

'We'd left the big yacht moored and gone in a small boat to explore some of Greece's smaller uninhabited islands. Anders was on the boat when I did a bad dive and hit my head on a rock. I resurfaced but I remember the blood streaming in my eyes. I remember it hurt. I remember I called to him.'

Zara watched him steadily. 'What did he do?'

'He was only fourteen, Zara,' he said huskily. 'Maybe he was frozen with fear.' He'd wanted to believe that. He didn't want to believe he'd truly seen such malevolence in someone so young. That chill filled his body. 'I thought he was holding the boat hook out for me to grab. But he didn't hold it still for me to reach for it. Instead, he hit down with it.'

'Hit *you*?'

'Right on the wound. At first I thought he'd lost control of the hook. But he hit again and then I just dived.

I swam underwater to get around a rocky outcrop so I could get away from him. My plan was to get to a beach, find someone somehow and phone for help. But on the other side of those rocks I got caught in a current and got carried out for miles.'

He paused and took a breath. He refused to think of this often. Now he remembered why. He'd been cold. And alone.

Zara put her hand on his wrist. To his amazement, he didn't flinch. Instead, he covered her hand with his and kept it there.

'How did you survive in the sea?' she asked.

'I was lucky enough to grab a bit of driftwood. I was hauled out of the water almost twenty hours later by a fisherman in a small boat. Miles from where I'd started. I was just lucky that the water hadn't been any colder.'

But it had been dark and he'd been terrified for too long.

'I think he thought I was an illegal migrant and he was certainly illegally fishing so we were both happy not to call the authorities. He stitched my split head back together. My eyes were swollen so much when I looked in a mirror that I didn't recognise myself. I was confused but conscious that I was in trouble. I stayed on that boat a couple of days but I knew I needed to get somewhere safe.'

'Piri-nu.'

'Niko, right.'

'How did you get all that way?'

'With difficulty. I managed to get a message to him using a satellite phone and stupid schoolboy code we'd developed at school. Niko sent transportation.'

But by the time he'd made it to Piri-nu infection and exhaustion had set in.

'I collapsed just after I made it there,' he admitted harshly. 'The only thing I managed to tell him was to stay silent about finding me. And he did. But it took me more than a fortnight to battle the pneumonia and while I was unconscious my mother rapidly deteriorated. Niko didn't know about that—the palace kept it quiet. She died before I came through.'

'Lucian...'

He couldn't stand to hear her softness.

'Niko had lost his own mother a few years earlier so he understood the impact of what he had to tell me. He was devastated that he'd not been able to get me home or to get a message to her before she went. But her passing was so sudden. As if any of it were his fault.'

'I'm so sorry, Lucian.'

He shook his head. It had all been his own damned fault. 'It took a lot to get my strength back. By then Garth had taken over as Regent for Anders. I knew I wasn't...*fit*.' Not physically, not mentally or morally. 'It would still be years before my possible coronation and at first I thought Garth might be best for Monrayne in the interim. I decided to get well and keep watch from afar and see.'

He couldn't look at her as he admitted how he'd let his country down. He couldn't tell her that he'd been paralysed with guilt about his mother's death. About his own part in her isolation at the end. He didn't deserve Zara's sympathy but right now he didn't want to lose the comfort of her hand under his.

'I kept tabs on all avenues for information and unfortunately in recent years the whisperings began.

There were rumblings about corruption with Garth. But worse was one story about Anders abusing a woman. Then another. I knew things he'd done as a boy. His cruelty to a stray puppy. His temper tantrums. And when I read his account of the accident he'd lied. He said I went overboard in the afternoon. I didn't. It was the morning. And he just waited for hours and hours before raising the alarm.' He gazed into Zara's white face. 'I couldn't let you marry him.'

'I know,' she whispered. 'Not me. Not anyone. And you couldn't let him become King.'

Her acknowledgement didn't soothe—it scoured deep inside. It was his fault that accident had happened at all. It had been his selfish desire to be on *holiday* and not in Monrayne, helping his unwell mother. He wasn't fit to be King when he'd been self-indulgent and inattentive. But he would be a better King than Anders and he would work to be even better still. He could only do that with rigorous, single-minded focus.

Zara was right. He didn't trust people now. But the person he trusted least was himself. Which was exactly why he couldn't give her everything she wanted from him.

Because he wasn't really worthy of his Crown and he wasn't worthy of her either.

CHAPTER NINE

LUCIAN UNEXPECTEDLY APPEARED in the library in the middle of the next day, carrying a laptop.

'Your sister has been in contact.' His gaze was unreadable. 'Apparently they haven't heard from you and now she's accusing me of holding you hostage or something outrageous.'

'Has she confused you with Anders?' Zara tried to laugh.

He leaned close and took her chin in his hand, making her look up at him. For such a big, strong man his touch was so tender, his voice soft. 'She wants to know where you are and how you are. The question is: do *you* want her to know these things?'

'It's taken them more than a week to remember my existence.' She'd deliberately not reached out to them. She'd wanted to see how long it would be until they tried to contact her. And yes, that was a little petty, perhaps, but she'd been deeply hurt.

'I'll scare her off if you want me to.'

She smiled but shook her head. She couldn't hide from her family for ever. Lucian had said she was courageous and right this second she believed him. After all, she'd stood up to him multiple times and he was the biggest, most intimidating person she'd ever met.

'Of course I'll take the call,' she said softly. 'Let's do it now.'

It took only moments for him to set up the link. Then he turned and shot her a bracing look. 'Don't let her get you down, Zara. Don't let her hurt you.'

'Even though she already has?' she challenged him. 'I'm *desperately* hurt, Lucian. Not by Anders, but by them. Absolutely. So why shouldn't I be honest? Why shouldn't I let her know how they've made me feel?'

He frowned as he stepped away.

'Will you stay in here?' she asked quickly.

He stopped, his eyebrow quirked. 'You would like that?'

She wasn't completely brave. She would like his support some more.

'To ensure your own reputation is protected, don't you think you should?'

He immediately took the seat diagonal from hers. 'The only thing I'm interested in protecting right now is you.'

Just like that, he stole her heart completely.

'Where are you?' her sister Ana asked as soon as Zara took her off mute.

'Still in Monrayne, as you obviously suspected.'

Ana's eyes rounded. 'Is he keeping you captive there?'

'Oh, no. If anything, it's the opposite,' Zara said. 'I forced him to let me stay.'

'I don't think anyone can make King Lucian do anything he doesn't want to,' Ana said.

Zara stiffened at the patronising tone. 'Did you know about Anders?'

Had her family been willing to allow her to marry a monster just for the money and prestige? Why had they abandoned her when she'd already been jilted? Their excuse that there might be unrest and therefore they might've been endangered was simply pitiful. Surely they could have cared about *her* safety—not just their own?

'Of course not,' Ana said impatiently.

Were they afraid that the truth now emerging about Anders somehow tarnished them too? Or that Lucian would somehow step in?

'You need to hurry up and come home,' Ana said. 'You know you're better off here. Mum and Dad miss you.'

They missed her so much they'd not bothered to get in touch. The fact was, her family simply didn't care enough about her. She'd tried to work out an escape route that would please them at the same time. She'd hoped to finally be of value to them *somehow.* But she obviously wasn't. At least now she knew for sure.

'I'm not coming back,' Zara said firmly. 'I'm re-nouncing my title.'

'What?' Ana almost screeched.

But Zara's attention flicked to the side. She caught Lucian's expression before it became stony again, but she knew she'd startled him.

'I don't want to be a princess any more,' she said more confidently. 'I'm going to be an ordinary citizen and live somewhere else entirely.'

'But—'

'I don't want to live in Dolrovia. I'll be back to

visit, of course. Quite soon.' Her parents were old and her father an invalid and, despite everything, she still loved them. She always would. But she was going to live her own life. 'You don't have to worry about me. I just want a quiet existence. I'm going to keep my head down. I'll be fine.'

'Are you going to do that in Monrayne?'

She hesitated and this time she didn't look for Lucian's reaction.

'No. This is a stepping stone until the media storm blows over.'

It felt amazingly good to say it. She literally felt lighter. No more princess. It was a powerfully liberating thought.

'What about us—the family, your country? Your duty to them both?'

'You don't actually need me. I've tried to do everything they wanted or what I thought they wanted and it didn't work out. Now I want to do something just for me.'

Ana sounded shocked. 'What about *money*?'

'I'll earn it,' she answered. 'Plenty of people do, you know.' And honestly it would be easier without the 'Princess' title. 'For now I'm going to have a holiday here, hiding away from the total humiliation. I'll be in touch again once I'm settled overseas.'

Zara avoided looking at Lucian long as she lowered the laptop screen. She still felt liberated but there was a moment of sadness. It was her family she was walking away from. But she needed the separation—at least while she recalibrated her own role within it and while she created a full life for herself.

'No more Princess?' Lucian said calmly.

'No.' She smiled. 'You know it's only an honorific anyway. Frankly, it's been more hindrance than help.'

'Do you know where you're going to go?'

She swallowed. 'I think England. There's lots of old historic homes that need administrators…'

'You want to do that?'

'I think I could, yes. I actually like the antiques and the art that tend to come with old country piles and I like the skill in the craft and the ancient architecture and making sure it survives.'

'Okay.' He nodded. 'But you think this is a *holiday* for you?'

She gave him a wan smile. 'I'm trying to make the best of a bad situation.'

He moved closer, his gaze almost tender. 'Then maybe we should make it even better.'

Her heart skipped. But he didn't pull her into his arms.

'Perhaps you should see some of *Monrayne's* ancient architecture before you go,' he said.

She shook her head, struggling to mask her disappointment. 'I don't want to be seen in public yet. Definitely not here.'

'Why, Zara—' he raised his scarred eyebrow at her '—are you not aware that I am a master of disguise?'

She giggled. 'Sunglasses aren't going to cut it in this case, Lucian.'

Lucian wished he was wearing his sunglasses right now. The luminescence of her hurt his eyes and maintaining an emotionless expression in the face of what he'd just heard was impossible.

She was leaving. Renouncing her title. Refusing her royal status. Ms All-or-Nothing was in action. And though he shouldn't be shocked by her decision, though he respected it, that old anger returned. Only it wasn't cold, it was hot, pure *frustration*. He knew she couldn't stay yet he didn't want her to leave. And how was she going to get to England? Who would she apply to for work—did she want a letter of introduction or support? Was she going to ask him to help her? He would in a heartbeat, of course.

But it was going to hurt like hell to do so.

So he turned his attention to something else— snatching at a weak idea while he settled the roiling emotion inside.

'You haven't seen some of the most beautiful parts of Monrayne. Some of our most stunning buildings. We'll get Victor to arrange it. You must at least go to the thermal springs.'

She flushed. 'Are you going to come with me?'

The invitation in her eyes bit deep. 'I can't, Zara.'

'You don't want to take a little respite? You've not stopped since your return. Not had a weekend—not even a single day.'

'No.' He ground out the refusal. 'The press would be onto you in a flash if I was with you.'

'Oh.' Her face fell. 'Yes, of course.'

But she'd wanted him with her and that made the temptation even harder to resist.

'You can bathe in the waters. Have a massage.' He almost choked at the thought. 'Eat what you want, do what you want.'

'A spa day at last,' she mock marvelled. 'What have I done to deserve such a reward?'

He gave in and pulled her close. 'Careful, Princess. Or I will demand payment.'

Her gaze turned smoky. 'What would you have me do?'

The willingness in her eyes almost undid him completely.

'You would like that, wouldn't you?' he said huskily.

He felt her trembling and knew the desire was as fierce for her as it was for him. But he resisted teasing her. He didn't even kiss her. At last he gave in to her insistence that there must be nothing between them. Because he was a breath away from taking the alternate deal—taking *everything* she offered.

'It can't happen,' he muttered, closing his eyes in sheer frustration, reminding himself more than he was telling her. 'You deserve so much better, Zara.'

She deserved someone who could give her all his attention.

But he had to be fully focused on his country. He'd promised himself he would on his mother's memory. He released her and walked away before she could argue. He'd go dwell in an ice-cold shower. For ever.

Early the next morning he was en route to a town a couple of hours' north of the capital. Zara's car was heading in a similar direction but would stop sooner. She was so pale. Some fresh air, sunlight—even winter sunlight—would benefit her. He wished he could join her as she bathed in those private, natural thermal springs. But this restorative experience was just for her. At least she would have it.

His day dragged and he was annoyed with himself for wondering about her when these people had waited so long to see him. So when he finally returned to the palace he hurriedly strode to their private wing. She should be back already. But the library was empty. So was the dining room.

'Where is Zara?'

Victor looked at him warily. 'There was an accident on the off ramp. The car was—'

Lucian stilled completely. The only word he retained in his head was *accident*. The last flicker of brain capacity tried to listen more, tried to... But his heart suddenly hammered, too hard, too fast, too loud. His throat tightened. A monster had its claws around his neck. He couldn't breathe.

Terror silenced him. Deafened him. All but immobilised him.

'Sir—?'

He stumbled as he forced his feet to move. *Alone.* He needed to be alone. To breathe.

She should have been back already. She should be telling him about the steaming waters. Instead, her rooms were empty. And he couldn't *consider* the word accident. He couldn't let himself think anything along those lines.

He needed to get to her. He needed to know she was okay. He needed that *now*. But, almost blind, it was all he could do to walk through the palace, feeling a sickening threat like no other until he came to the most central, most secure of rooms. Secure as a bank vault, it was dimly lit and had reinforced walls. Silence. Space. Safety.

He would wait there, uselessly holding his aching head.

He closed the door behind him then stared, aghast,

at the empty gold throne that seemed to mock him. He was so weak. He couldn't think. He couldn't move. How could he ever be King when he reacted like this to just a word?

CHAPTER TEN

ZARA WENT STRAIGHT to the dining room, her stomach rumbling. She hoped Lucian hadn't finished already, she wanted to tell him all about her day. But he wasn't there. Silver domes still covered the many dishes and Victor looked tense as he stood to attention.

'Has Lucian eaten?' she asked him.

The servant shook his head.

'Has he not come home yet?'

'He got back some time ago,' Victor said, almost hesitantly. 'He's been in the throne room since his return.'

Zara nodded. 'Is he in a meeting?'

'I believe he's alone, ma'am.'

Zara was unwilling to ask the servant anything personal about the King, but there was something meaningful in the way the man was now hovering beside her with an unusually worried expression.

'Perhaps I'll see if he's ready to dine,' Zara muttered.

Her heart skittered as she walked to the throne room. She knew it was in the very centre of the palace, a relic of the original castle that had been built here and added to over the centuries. It wasn't massive but the stone walls were thick and the steel door heavy and hard to open. A couple of side lights cast a minimal glow, yet even so the throne on the dais glittered. But it stood empty. The surrounding velvet drapery looked heavy and lush.

She peered in the dimness. Then she saw a movement in the shadows—his back was against the wall in the furthest corner of the room. She stepped in and let the heavy door seal shut behind her before speaking softly. 'Lucian?'

She heard his sudden sharp inhalation—an alarmingly rough gasp for air.

'Has something happened?' She hurried towards him.

She stared as she neared because his mouth moved but no sound emerged. But it was obvious what he'd tried to say—*Zara*.

'Lucian?'

He sighed—a huge release of tension.

'Go.' This time his voice was audible. A low, ragged growl. And the distress in his eyes was very real.

She swallowed. 'No.'

He flinched and his breathing became choppier.

She took a steadying breath of her own. Here, in this heart of the palace, there were no windows and only that one door. She instinctively understood that that was why he'd come here. He'd needed safety. She just didn't know why.

'I won't talk to you. I won't touch you. But I will *not* leave you alone. Not when you're obviously upset.' She bit her lip. She was desperate to reach for him but she didn't.

Storm clouds swirled in his eyes—she wasn't sure

he could even see her properly. Sweat slicked his brow.
His hands curled into even tighter fists. His chest rapidly rose and fell as he stared at her. She waited where
she'd stopped, just a few feet from him. As he stared
at her his breathing slowly eased.

'Zara.'

His voice was still rough and she couldn't tell if he
was using her name as a curse or a prayer.

But she didn't answer. She'd said she wouldn't talk
and she wouldn't break his trust. Not ever.

'I need you to tell me you're okay,' he muttered.

'Of course I'm—'

'There was an accident,' he interrupted harshly.

He knew that?

'It was nothing,' she said quickly. 'We got rear-
ended on the way back. But it was barely a knock. I'm
fine, so are both drivers.'

His breath hissed. 'Come closer,' he growled. 'Let
me see.'

She moved before he changed his mind, stopping a
mere breath from him.

His hands still shook as he framed her face—tilting
it one side to the other so he could see better in what
little light there was. And she saw better too—the concern in his eyes, the tension in his face. She realised
the truth and it rent her heart.

'You were worried about me,' she whispered.

He stared into her eyes and his breathing rough-
ened again.

'Lucian,' she added even more softly. 'It's okay. I'm
fine.'

But his hands gently searched. Carefully he probed
her neck, her shoulders, down her arms—feeling for

himself that she was unharmed. Even more gently, he then swept the sides of her ribs, her waist…

Her breathing began to quicken. He was merely checking she was unharmed but she was becoming aroused. She'd missed him today. She was going to miss him for ever soon. And she just wanted—

'I need to see you,' he growled.

His hands were on her collarbone and he looked directly into her eyes. That was when she saw the fire now building in his. The fire that matched her own. She nodded and the next second he ripped the front of her dress apart.

'I cannot resist you,' he groaned as his gaze dipped to her chest.

'Why do you want to?'

'I don't know any more. I don't know anything any more. I just need you. I need to feel you.'

He cupped her bra. Her breasts felt heavy and she simply melted—pressing right against him. Because he was like a furnace and she was cast deep into his fiery passion. His hands slid around her ribs. He unfastened the strap and took her bra off completely before returning his attention to her now bared breasts. Skin on skin. She gasped at the gentle sweep of his thumbs across her nipples and shivered at the smile that then curved his mouth.

'Zara…'

He lowered her to the floor and joined her there. Her dress was in a puddle about them, while unbuttoning his shirt was almost impossible because he was so intent on kissing every inch of her. He removed her panties and slid the remnants of her dress up to her waist and kissed every inch he exposed in the process.

The intimacy was searing. He kissed her so wickedly that she groaned. But she wasn't ashamed at how hot she was already. She felt the thickness of his arousal pressing against her and knew it was the same for him. There was this between them. There had been from the beginning. When she'd been supposed to be marrying another man she'd turned in that cathedral and seen him and it had been like a bolt of lightning. So hey, she wasn't perfect either. But he'd held back for all these nights.

She reached for him. 'Are you sure?' she whispered.

'I want this. With *you*,' he growled, rising to lie between her legs.

He was heavy and she trembled with the delight of having him press against her so fully, so intimately.

She framed his face with her hand, feeling the heat of his skin. 'You were upset. I'm sorry you were so worried.'

'I haven't had a panic attack like that in a very long time.'

'You're very tired. You have so much going on. Maybe it isn't right to make this choice now...' She bit her lip but she had to make sure *he* was sure. 'I couldn't stand it if you were to regret this.'

'Regret is my constant companion,' he muttered hoarsely. 'I've regretted not doing this every night since we met. I wanted you the minute I saw you in that cathedral. I've only wanted you more with every day since.'

Stunned, she stared up at him.

'I'm tired of fighting how much I want you.' He pressed his pelvis against her to prove his point. 'I'm tired of not giving in to what I *really* want.'

And that was this. With her. She felt it in his straining muscles, in the care with which he kissed her and caressed her, she felt it in the huge erection digging against her now. And she could never resist because she wanted him too. To be so very much wanted was everything.

'Lucian,' she whispered.

She wriggled her hands between them and unfastened his trousers. He closed his eyes as she wrapped her fingers around his girth. She stroked him tentatively at first, then with increasing grip and pleasure as she watched his unfettered reaction.

'I'm really selfish, Zara,' he muttered through gritted teeth. 'I want *everything*.'

'Then take it.'

He gripped her wrist, stopping her strokes and lifting her hand away. He dropped his hips onto hers and she felt the hard head of him pressing against her slick seam. Then he thrust. Hard.

They both groaned—guttural and raw—as he breached her body at last. She met his gaze. They swapped a breath. Then swapped a smile. And both of them slid into a mingled sigh as he thrust again, even deeper. He was right there, absolutely inside her. It was so intimate. It was everything.

'Zara…' His passionate whisper echoed so deeply within her.

She swept her hands over his broad shoulders. In his huge pupils she saw wonder—despite that storm of emotion before. Yet another storm brewed now. Emotion of an altogether different kind. Hunger and need and the determination to satisfy and be satisfied. Nothing less than everything would sate either of them.

'Don't hold back.' She instinctively arched, encouraging him to ride her.

'I won't,' he muttered.

And then he proved it—covering her mouth with his as he moved. He was so strong. So intent. And it was so good. Every atom within her quivered. It was all she could do to kiss him back, to hold him close, to wrap her arms and legs around him and cling as he surged into her.

'Zara—'

'*Yes. Yes!*' She let go and let desire swamp her entirely.

He growled and pumped furiously, utterly lost in her embrace. She revelled in the fever glazing his eyes and the need bunching his muscles. She was as incomprehensible, as uncontrolled as she arched to meet him with every muscle, loving the ferocity of their dance until they slammed into that end point, shuddering through tumultuous wave after wave of orgasm.

Long minutes later they were a loosened tangle of limbs, torn clothing and sweat but still intimately, deeply entwined. Zara never wanted to move again. But slowly their breathlessness ebbed and her wariness prickled.

'I'm too heavy,' he muttered with a small smile. But still several long moments passed before he finally summoned the strength to lift away to sit beside her with his back against the wall. Maybe he needed to be able to see the door, but his alert gaze was utterly focused on her. That smile turned rueful.

'We will marry immediately,' he said huskily.

'We will not,' she whispered sadly. That wasn't what either of them wanted. Especially him.

'You might be pregnant,' he pointed out. 'We just had unprotected sex.'

'I won't be pregnant,' she muttered obstinately.

'Sometimes it only takes the once.'

She looked at him. 'I'm on the pill.'

'What?' His eyes dilated and she felt him tense. 'That's impossible. Weren't you supposed to provide Anders with an heir?'

'Yeah, well, I wanted to wait a few months to see what married life was like first. I didn't want to get pregnant instantly like some brood mare. And most of all I wanted to control my cycle so I wasn't struggling up the aisle with cramps and a bloated belly. Call me vain, I don't care. There were so many cameras in there.'

He stared at her. 'Then we won't have a public ceremony. Ours can be private.'

'*We* will not have *any* kind of ceremony.' She shook her head. '*You* will give them a whole public performance with the perfect princess bride eventually. In a decade, right? But not with me. I'm never facing that scrutiny again, not after—' She broke off bitterly. 'Not even for you.'

She felt the crush inside at what her words had given away—*not even for you*. And, besides, it wasn't true. She would put on another stupidly sparkly dress and stand in front of millions all over again if he really wanted her to…but the point was he didn't really want that. He'd thought he had to ask in case he'd just got her pregnant. But he didn't want to get married for a decade. He'd made that more than clear. She suspected he didn't really want to ever marry anyone at all.

'But if you *are* pregnant—'

'We'd have to be extremely unlucky.' But her heart twisted. In her world it wouldn't be unlucky at all. Except while he wanted her, he wasn't in *love* with her. And she couldn't be in love with him, right?

'Stranger things have happened.'

She shook her head. 'No, Lucian.'

He glanced down at her. 'Your dress is ruined. I'm sorry.'

'I don't give a damn about my dress. And don't you dare apologise for ruining anything *else*. That was the most sublime experience of my life and you're not wrecking it with your regrets.' She threw her arm over her face so she didn't have to see him and he couldn't see her. 'Take them and leave.'

She heard him draw in a deep steadying breath. 'Zara—'

'You are *not* ruining the last of my afterglow.'

'Fine.'

To her surprise, he half laughed.

'I will not ruin the last of your afterglow,' he said. 'I'm very glad you have an afterglow.'

She kept her face covered, still unwilling to see his face as she asked, 'Do you?'

'I'm pretty sure those astronauts up in the international space station can see my afterglow.'

She lowered her arm and looked at his gorgeous smile and her tension melted all over again. 'Through the stone walls and everything?'

'Absolutely. I don't have any regrets about this, Zara.

Not *ever*.' He gazed at her and his chest rose and fell that bit quicker again. 'You're amazing. That was amazing.'

Lucian watched her skin flush more enchantingly than ever. She swallowed hard and turned her gaze up towards the beautiful ceiling of the throne room.

'It's a beautiful palace,' she said eventually.

'Yes.'

'You missed it?'

'More than I realised.' He ached to be worthy of it. And, for this fleeting moment, worthy of her. In this one impossible moment he wanted everything.

She'd just seen him—held him—at his most animal. When instinct had overridden reason and the desire of the flesh had won. They'd assuaged that relentless ache and he could never regret it. Mind blown. Body broken. Yet he felt energised in an altogether new way. It was wonderful.

If she was lying about being on birth control—and he truly didn't think she was—then she might get pregnant. And, heaven help him, in this moment he didn't care. He, who'd vowed not to have children for years, would demand she marry him. She wouldn't be able to say no, and part of him would be *pleased*. Here was the horrible truth. He was greedy. A selfish monster who would not let her go. Who took what he wanted—uncaring of the impact of his actions on anyone else. He was as spoiled as his poisonous cousin and arrogant with it. Because he knew that was not what she wanted.

She wanted to renounce her title. She didn't want pomp and pageantry—she didn't want to live the kind of life he would have as King. She knew too well it came with peril. She'd only entertained the idea of mar-

rying Anders because she'd thought it was her only way
of escaping her home. But she had another option now.
So he couldn't coerce her into something different.

He couldn't bear to think of those moments when
he'd thought she'd been hurt. He couldn't relive it.
Couldn't stand to analyse why it had almost destroyed
him. Maybe it was just that he was overtired. But he
couldn't resist running his hand down her arm, needing to touch her while he could.

She turned her head towards him. 'I can't believe
you've never done that before,' she said softly. 'I can't
believe *I've* never done that before.' She smiled a little
sadly. 'We've been missing out.'

'We have.' His whole body ached to have her again.

An impish look lit her eyes. 'So when *did* you learn
how to please a woman?'

He chuckled. 'I might have fooled around back when
I was a senior at school.'

'Before you disappeared.'

'Yes. But I'd not quite got to have the full experience.'

She caressed his jaw and a smug look entered her
eyes. 'I'm glad.'

He leaned into the soft touch—a balm he knew he
couldn't indulge in for long. 'You're right to say no to
marrying me,' he muttered. 'I'm not good enough for
you, Zara.'

'Why do you say that?'

He kept silent for a few more moments, but in the
end he was so tired and felt so accepted by her that the
miserable truth simply came out.

'I meant it when I told you I was selfish. I truly am
and that's what drives me to do better now. My mother

was dying of cancer and I chose to go away on holiday instead of spending time with her. Instead of easing her burden I made it much worse.'

Zara's beautiful eyes widened. 'Lucian——'

'Listen.' Now he'd started he needed her to understand everything. He needed her to want to walk away from him because he wasn't entirely sure he could let her go now. 'My father died in a car accident when I was four. My mother buried her heart with him. She devoted her life to her country and to me. She was loving and generous. That's why she opened up the palace to Anders and Garth.'

'She was kind.'

'And loyal like no one else. She would have done anything for us. I had the opposite upbringing to you, Zara—I had full prince privileges. Almost everything I wanted, I got. I'd been away at boarding school—clueless about the burden of the Crown and wrapped up in my own late teen life. I was looking forward to starting my degree. I thought I had the world at my feet.

I hadn't seen that much of her, but I did notice she was thinner and she seemed more tired. I thought she was just older. I didn't consider the details as closely as I should have. It was a surprise to me when she asked me to defer going to university for a year and shadow her working in the stateroom. I realise now that perhaps she knew her time was limited and she wanted to train me while she could. But I wasn't gracious in my acceptance of her request. My trade-off was to have one last holiday. I insisted on it like the spoilt little prince I was.'

'Had she told you she was unwell?'

He sucked in a painful breath. 'Only right before

I left. Because she asked me to take Anders with me. You can imagine I wasn't enthused. That's when she said she wasn't well—a small tumour, she said. I was shocked and didn't ask the right questions. I made some noises about not going, but she said she wanted to see both Anders and me have a nice break together before we got to work. So we went.' He frowned. 'It was ovarian cancer. They found it late, but there could have been more time. There should have been. But when I went missing the stress destroyed her. It was so fast, Zara. It monstered her.'

He couldn't bear to think of his mother lying so unwell and so alone. He should have been there to support her.

'She'd already lost so much. It's unfathomable to me how Anders could put her through more when she'd given him so much. But I'd been just as cruel. I'd been careless and self-centred. And the truth is I'm still not who I need to be. I'm not a worthy heir to her Crown. And I'm not the man for you.'

'You don't think you're being a little hard on yourself?' Zara said quietly. 'What teenager hasn't been the centre of their own universe? What young adult hasn't wanted to go on holiday at the beach?'

'If I hadn't made that choice then the accident wouldn't have happened. My mother wouldn't have died sooner than she should have and even more heartbroken, as she did.'

'You're not blaming yourself for your own attempted murder, are you? Or for the death of your mother from cancer? You're powerful, Lucian, but not *that* powerful.'

'I lacked critical judgement. My choice set in motion a cascade of events, and it hastened her death. She suffered greatly and it was utterly avoidable.'

'And that was Anders's fault, not yours.'

Zara was heartbroken for him. 'It sounds to me like she wanted you to go have that last summer of fun.' She paused. 'But now you don't allow yourself that. Is this why you live a life of personal denial? Because you think you don't deserve it?'

'Because I need to put my duty *first*,' he corrected. 'I need to remain focused on Monrayne. That's my vow—the decade I was away is the decade the country gets. Fully focused. By then I'll be better at it. Because I know that when I get distracted by personal wants or impulses, my choices aren't always wise. Look at me now...'

Yes, this wasn't wise.

'None of us make wise choices all of the time. We're not perfect, remember? Don't you think you deserve to have it all at some time in the future?' she asked. 'I want that for me. You should want that for you too.'

He shook his head. 'I can't fail my country. Or my mother's memory.'

'You're worried you can't live up to her. You already do, Lucian. You're a good King. You're a good listener.'

'You're wrong. I didn't listen closely enough to her. And I didn't see how bad Anders was becoming.'

'Because you were young too. And his betrayal was a shocking, terrible thing. Realising that someone you thought you knew was nothing like you imagined, that they're capable of cruelty... It makes you doubt everything. *Especially* yourself.'

She felt disillusioned by her own family. She'd been

willing to do what was asked of her. She'd supported them. Yet they'd not stayed to support her. And that hurt. Desperately. Lucian had been left alone too. He had lost his family. His country. His sense of purpose. His belief in his ability to do and be what his job required. So he'd not come back for a while, and she didn't blame him.

'You didn't come back for revenge. You came back for *redemption*,' she realised. 'But you're already a worthy King, Lucian. You might have made youthful mistakes but you're more than good enough as you are. You can do your job and have an actual life. You shouldn't carry this burden and you don't have to sacrifice anything else. You should have everything. In fact you'll be a better King if you do.'

He was silent. She realised he disagreed. He was punishing himself for perceived failures from so long ago and he wouldn't change his mind on what he believed he needed to do. His decade of duty. He would stick to his plan.

She had to do the same. She had to reach for what she'd long wanted, and that was her independence. Getting further entangled with Lucian would only risk that.

'I'm not sorry we did this, but I think we both know we can't do it again,' she whispered.

He looked at her sombrely. 'Zara—'

She silenced him with a shake of her head. 'You need to focus on your duty and I need to find my freedom.'

Instinct told her that if she stayed much longer her heart would be trapped here for good. He had such a complete effect on her.

'So once we leave this room?'

'It ends. We both have things that need our full attention.'

'You don't want this to become an affair now? You said yourself you're not going to be here long.'

She reached for the courage he'd told her she had and whispered the uncomfortable truth. 'I'm scared I'll end up wanting more. And that can't happen.' Even though she had the horrible feeling it might already have. 'It's just really bad timing, Lucian.'

He stared at her with such intensity her too-vulnerable heart melted. She had to stop this conversation now. She couldn't expose herself any more than she just had.

'But we haven't left this room *yet*,' she muttered in one last surrender. 'And I've not yet seen you fully naked…'

He suddenly swooped.

'Lucian—'

'Indulge me,' he said huskily. Lifting her into his arms, he carried her to the throne. 'I don't want to crush you. I want to see you too.'

He set her on her feet and quickly stripped them both of the last clothes tangled between them. Then he sat back on the throne and lifted her again so she straddled his lap. That meant she got an up close and wonderful view of his chest. As he did of hers. And that meant there was then a battle of playful kisses and nips and tweaks and tongues until in the end there was only wild movement and absolute abandonment. Again.

And then—even when they were exhausted and sweaty—again. It was a slow, aching indulgence and so tender her eyes watered. She had to close them to hide the tears from him. But he knew anyway because she couldn't seem to hide anything from him. He simply cradled her close and neither spoke a word.

It was a long, *long* time later before she pulled the remnants of her dress back on. She paused at the door and glanced to where he remained sprawled alone in that massive chair, needing to admit one last truth of her own.

'I'll always be glad I did this with you first, Lucian.'

CHAPTER ELEVEN

THE ANGER WAS BACK. She was pleased she'd done that with him first, was she? The predator within him wanted to be her *first* and *only* and *always*. But he couldn't be. He knew with his brain that Zara was right in calling a halt to any affair before it had really begun. His blood, however, was dead certain she was wrong.

She'd been so brave—leaving her home, prepared to make a deal in the hope of a better life; resilient in the face of public rejection and the worse private rejection of her family; courageous in standing up to him and saying what she needed. She was tough. He wished she would take a little more solace—steal a little more pleasure—with him. Yes, in these weak moments he changed his mind completely. He ached for more time alone with her. Fortunately for him, she was strong—determined to maintain her new boundaries. Because she *was* leaving and what they shared was perhaps too intense.

She was right about other things too. He *had* denied himself pleasure all this time. And didn't it serve him right that the one woman he now wanted was unavailable to him? Because, of course, he would respect her decision. This was a woman who needed agency. To take control of her own life. She wanted her independence. But Princess All-or-Nothing had twisted that on him again in the most frustrating way.

Yet thank goodness she had, because he had that lifetime of work ahead of him. But, in truth, his return to claim the Crown had gone better than he'd ever imagined it would. He was extremely busy but there was no crisis in the country. He just had to stay calm and stick to the plan. Keep going. Step by step. And that meant not seducing Zara again. That meant regaining his self-control entirely.

Monrayne now needed global recognition of its stability and he knew exactly how to prove that. The next day he visited another town and then lost track of time in planning after his return. Which meant he was very late for dinner by the time he realised the hour. Naturally she'd long left the dining room so he went searching and found her in the library, sorting through the never-ending letters now that she'd finished with the books.

'You dined without me,' he said mock-balefully.

'Did you expect me to wait when you were so very late?' she countered archly.

'Of course not. I wouldn't dream of making you go hungry, Princess.' He was unable to resist a little verbal tease. He didn't think it possible for them to end that altogether.

She shot him a look. 'And I haven't.' Her smile widened to the point that a dimple appeared in her cheek. 'I even have some supper.' She gestured with her hand and he saw a laden tray on the table behind her. 'Would you like to share?' she asked blandly.

Their favourite displacement activity again? He promptly sat down.

Zara nudged the tray nearer. 'I'm sure you must be hungry. You don't eat when you're on show.'

He mustered a faint smile. 'I genuinely don't feel hungry when I'm out there.'

'I know.' She nodded in complete acceptance. 'You're concentrating hard on everything else. Knowing everyone's names, keeping tabs on what they're all doing and saying.'

He nodded. That was exactly it.

'So have something to eat now.' She picked up a piece of cheese and bit into it with a cheeky smile. 'Before I eat it all.'

'Temptress,' he jeered softly.

'I do try.'

He leaned unnecessarily close to her as he reached to select a small slice of tart. 'I wish you really would.'

The look she shot him then was sharper. He chuckled as he chewed. The bone-deep weariness morphed into an aching cross between contentment and yearning. He was *relaxed*, with another person present— frankly, a miracle. But it was *because* of the other person present. Only he wanted more from her still.

'I'm going to hold a ball.' He told her his plans to keep himself on track. 'To show the world that the situation here in Monrayne has settled and that I'm here to stay. It seems a shame to waste the fireworks that were planned for Anders's celebrations.'

'Your coronation ball?'

He tensed. 'Not the coronation. Not yet. Just a ball.'

'Is there reason to delay it?' Zara asked.

'Is there reason to rush it?' he countered.

'You still don't feel worthy?'

He drew a breath because she was so very acute and he never should have told her all that he had. 'I am King already, Zara, that pageant is purely ceremonial. Right now, I need to focus on doing the job and part of doing the job is showing the world that Monrayne is politically stable.'

'Monrayne is humming. I've seen it on the news— the place is filled with chatter and vibrancy. They're all clamouring to get closer and see you. It must be nice to know they're so happy you're back.'

He sighed. He knew he had to be seen and seen to be confident. 'It's important the world sees serenity, stability, security. That foreigners aren't afraid to visit. It's important for tourism and investment.'

'Will the guests you need come?'

'Niko will definitely be here.' Lucian smiled. Once the confirmation that Niko would attend was made public more acceptances would come quickly. Niko was popular at parties. 'I'd like you to attend as well.'

She froze. 'You're not serious.'

'You can't hide for ever,' he said softly. 'You need to show your face.'

'That's ironic, coming from you.'

'Quite. You have the benefit of learning from my mistakes. Nothing good comes from not facing your fears, Zara. You can't live the rest of your life hiding from what's happened.'

'Why not? I could just slip away to England, never to be seen on that public princess circuit again.'

'Aside from the wedding-that-wasn't, have you *ever* been on the public princess circuit?'

She stared at him reproachfully.

'No. You haven't,' he answered for her.

She should have had so much more. She should have had everything. *He* had. He'd had all the luxury experience of being born royal. He'd also had that time away in Piri-nu, out of the spotlight, where he'd had a physical freedom unlike any he'd experienced before and probably would never have again.

But Zara was a princess who'd never been enabled to enjoy any of the perks. She'd been short-changed. She'd had the restrictions without the rewards. She'd been more than hidden, she'd been ignored and isolated. So she should have a few moments of the fun that could be had. Because it wasn't all bad—far from it. It was an honour and privilege to meet the people he got to meet. And she'd never got to understand just what a natural she could be. As someone who could talk to literally anyone—who could set the most uncomfortable man in the world at ease—given the chance, he believed she could excel. Because she was a genuine sweetheart. He wanted her to understand that too.

'You can do this, Zara. You know it's just a party with fancier food than usual.'

'Stop trying to amuse me into acquiescence.'

'Shall I go with issuing a command instead?'

She swallowed. 'Why is it so important to you that I attend?'

He hesitated. 'Honestly, it would be helpful to me if you would come and keep King Niko's wife Maia company. She's very new to royal life. She hasn't been to plenty of palace receptions and could do with some support in an environment like this.'

'You really think I'm the right person for that task?'

'I think you're kind. And you're really good at filling strained silences.' He smiled at her. 'I think you understand how uncomfortable you can feel when you're not used to it.'

'Solidarity in awkwardness?' she asked. 'Will you invite anyone else from my family?'

'Not if you don't want me to. I think you can represent your family beautifully.'

'It can be my first ball and last official duty ever as a princess. But I don't want to be seen *with* you,' she said in a low voice. 'I don't want…'

Regret welled within him. 'I know. There will be no speculation about anything between us. You'll have returned from your sanctuary, that's all.'

There was no "them".

'People are going to stare at me,' she muttered.

'Maybe.' He adopted a teasing drawl. 'They'll stare at me more, though. So I'll stay on the other side of the room and distract them for you.'

At last she smiled. 'How very chivalrous of you.'

'I'll even go without my sunglasses so they can all unsubtly stare at my scar.'

Her smile grew. 'I don't think anything can surpass the bare chest in the cathedral moment.'

'You think I should wear something revealing?' He chuckled. 'Perhaps, just for you, I will.'

'Full drama, Lucian. I have to hand it to you.'

'So you'll go?'

'If you really want me to.'

'I do.' More than that, he wanted her to *enjoy* it. It mattered so much to him. That she wanted to turn her back on this life didn't sit right when she didn't really know what it could be like. 'You'll need support to get ready. I'll arrange a maid.'

He'd show her that she truly was a princess.

'I don't need a maid—' she laughed '—I've *never* had one.' She lifted her chin. 'I can manage on my own perfectly well. I can even put my own toothpaste on my own toothbrush.'

'All the essentials of life,' he teased.

'Quite. I might not be able to survive on the streets just yet, but I'm going to be fine on my own.'

He really didn't want to think about her leaving. Not yet. Even though he knew it would happen sooner rather than later. Even though he knew he was going to help her get away in the end. She hadn't asked him yet, but he knew he would fly her out of here when she did.

'Have you something you can wear to the ball?'

'Well…' She lit up. 'I do have this really big white dress that's only been worn once.'

'*Not* that.' He laughed. But he didn't want her wearing anything associated with Anders. None of those perfectly princess-appropriate dresses that Garth's minions had ordered either. 'I'll arrange something.'

'Given they're all going to be looking and judging me, that would be amazing and thank you. But please just rent something, you don't need to buy anything.' She wrinkled her nose. 'I definitely don't want another total makeover.'

'No? Hadn't we better get a beautician in for these horror nails?' He couldn't resist taking her hand.

'Not those scary assistants again,' she groaned.

'Someone else, I promise.'

'I'm not having them that ridiculous length again. And at least I'm not going to have to flash around some massive ring.'

'Such a relief not to have that burden,' he agreed

gravely and lifted her fingers to his mouth. 'You'll need some jewels though.'

He'd missed her softness. Her scent.

'I think my family vault has been depleted,' she muttered jerkily.

'This time you may borrow from me.' Something tightened in his gut at the thought of draping a chain of diamonds across her sensitive skin.

'Oh, no.' She shook her head. 'It would not be wise to wear *anything* associated with the Monrayne Royal family, given I've just been jilted by the Crown Prince,' she said caustically. 'Even if he is now a fugitive.'

'He's no longer Crown Prince.'

'That change in the law went through?'

'There was no objection to its speed either.' But Lucian wasn't satisfied on that score yet. He wanted Anders found and to face justice for the hurt he'd caused those women and who knew what other cruelties.

He drew a breath, focusing on what he could do here and now. And the one thing that he wanted that he could actually make happen was for Zara to attend the ball. 'So we'll find you something else to wear.'

'I don't need anything else.'

He rolled his eyes, annoyed with her rejection on many levels. 'You know that's not how these things work. You'll look all the more pitiful if you're in a plain ill-fitting number with no bling.' He paused and appealed to the pride he knew she had. 'You need a revenge dress.'

She looked at him for a second and then laughed with such amusement that he couldn't help but join her.

'Wow,' she breathed. 'Well, you are the King of

Revenge Dressing, what with the bare-chested cathedral moment.'

'And we're back to that.' His amusement—his attraction—soared.

'It isn't something I'm ever going to forget. Honestly, it was the highlight of that horrific day. The one thing that saved it.'

He faux flexed in response to the compliment. 'Aside from the small fact that you didn't end up marrying an absolute jerk.'

She sighed.

'And I remember other moments from later in that day that weren't so awful,' he added. 'Plus I know how to make you change your mind about certain things,' he said softly. 'All I have to do is take off my shirt.'

'Well now, that wouldn't be fair,' she whispered.

'Life isn't fair, Princess. You and I both know that already.'

'Which is why we respect each other's space.'

He read the conflicting emotions in her beautiful eyes. Slowly, reluctantly he released her hand. He noticed she slipped it beneath the table into her lap, a trembling fist.

He gritted his teeth as his delight evaporated. But he refused to regret all that had happened between them. Never those moments in the throne room, when that explosion of emotion had culminated in the most shattering experience of his life.

But if she came to this ball she would be back in society—possibly for the last time as a princess. And if she renounced her title, if she left and lived in England, she would meet other people. Other men. A *better* man than him, no doubt.

He glanced down and saw his own hands were curled into fists now. He made himself inhale. Exhale. Relax even, as he faced hard facts. She *couldn't* stay hidden here indefinitely. She had to go. She had to live her life as she wanted.

From the moment she entered that ballroom anything between them would be over.

CHAPTER TWELVE

ZARA DIDN'T WANT to be cast adrift in the ballroom alone, but it was a necessary moment for her to live through. Just to prove to herself that she could. To prove it to Lucian too. Though, in fairness, she knew he already believed in her. That he considered her brave gave her the lift she needed to take the final step inside.

It also helped that he'd imported a team from an eye-wateringly expensive Parisian fashion house to help her get ready. They'd signed a non-disclosure agreement and arrived armed with an assortment of couture, jewels and make-up. There'd been no need to be stitched into her gown this time. Nor was it a loud, overly ornate showstopper that she drowned inside.

It was a deep blue simple column that clung to some curves then fell in a silky sweep to the floor. The bodice rose right to the base of her throat, it was long-sleeved, high-backed. In fact it would be considered extremely demure if it weren't for the tiny buttons that ran from that high neckline to her narrow waist. The buttons were set beneath each other a few inches apart, while each half of the fabric they held was set the merest millimetre apart—so from her neck to her navel, all the way down her sternum, there were glimpses of skin exposed and no hiding the fact she wore no bra. Though one had to stand close to see *that*. The only jewels she wore were the sapphire earrings that had arrived in her rooms that afternoon. They were astonishingly light, unlike the heavy diamond drops from her failed wedding day.

The ripple that ran through the crowd as her entrance was announced was impossible to ignore. Unfortunately, most of the guests were already in place in the ballroom but it had taken longer for her hair to be done than she'd anticipated. Every last one turned to stare. She felt the familiar prickling sensation over her skin but kept her chin lifted. She wasn't going to hide the impact of her emotions on her body. She wasn't going to let herself down. And she was also here for Lucian. Serene and secure, like Monrayne itself.

She knew that tonight was essentially a dress rehearsal for his formal coronation in a few months and she wanted to do everything she could to help it be a success. He needed this—he needed belief in himself. Her presence was a symbol of healing—that he'd not done harm to her by interrupting her wedding.

The days before the ball had slid by too quickly. And throughout every one she'd regretted requesting that they not repeat the intimacy they'd shared in the throne room. But neither of them was in a position to have any kind of relationship. She was trying to be wise. But it was so very hard to be sensible when they'd still dined together each night. Still discussed the day. Still laughed. And perhaps that was the mistake. Because that was the connection they had—it wasn't only that earth-shattering sex. And even though she still saw him then, more and more she missed him terribly and she slept less and less.

After navigating the steep stairs and enduring everyone's eyes, she scanned the room. He stood with his back to the wall, ensuring he could visually check the ballroom in a single sweep. But right now his gaze was fixed on her. Even from this distance she felt his heat singeing her heart.

She made herself turn. Made herself do what she'd said she would.

'It's an honour to meet you, King Niko.' She curtseyed to the man who knew more about Lucian than anyone, nervous to make a good impression on him.

'Princess Zara.' He bowed and then turned. 'May I introduce my wife, Maia.'

The tenderness with which he drew the pretty woman forward tore Zara's heart a little. They chatted for a time—simple talk of differences in climate before a more honest smile about palace regulations. Other people came up to speak with them—though mostly with Niko. But eventually the more curious addressed Zara directly.

'You've had a very challenging time.' One loud woman openly stared at her.

'Indeed. But I feel very relieved,' Zara said softly. 'It seems I had a lucky escape.'

It was mortifying to have been so naive and ignorant of her fiancé's nature. To have been so gullible and then rejected so publicly, so brutally.

'Royal alliances can be complicated.' Niko stepped in smoothly. 'It will settle down, I'm sure.'

King Niko very clearly only had eyes for Maia but he turned to Zara intently, shielding her from the other people present. 'Though I do find it fascinating that you've remained here through this challenging time.'

What had Lucian told him? Zara licked her lips nervously.

'King Lucian has been very kind to me,' she said diplomatically.

'*Kind?*' Niko said in a low voice only Zara could hear. 'The Lucian I know isn't *kind*. He's austere in every element of his life. Fiercely and ruthlessly focused on his work.'

'Indeed, it is difficult to get him to talk of much else. But he *is* very kind.' She stoutly defended him to the one man she'd thought *would* know and appreciate Lucian's depths.

She couldn't help glancing across the ballroom towards the tall figure. She knew it was safe enough to do so. *Everyone* was watching him, all as fascinated as she. It wasn't just curiosity but the fact he was compelling. Not to mention unbearably handsome. But his ice-blue gaze was upon her right now and she stilled, feeling the heat rising within her. All she had to do was look at him and she was lost.

She quickly turned back.

Niko had leaned away to murmur something to Maia before they both smiled, but he then stepped back to her. 'Will you dance, Princess Zara?'

'Oh.' Her nervousness spiked. She hadn't thought she would dance at all. She'd half hoped to escape the ball early. She'd planned to show her face, hold her head high, stay just long enough to settle Maia in and then quietly leave once everyone had got over the surprise of seeing her present. Dancing would put her far more on show. Especially dancing with King Niko.

'Everyone is watching you anyway, Princess,' Niko said softly. 'Why not show them how little you care about what has happened?'

Men like Niko and Lucian were not used to being denied. Plus, she *was* a princess. She was supposed to dance at palace balls. And the truth was she never had. She'd never been to a ball like this.

'Thank you, it would be an honour.'

He bowed and led her onto the dance floor. She was aware of most people turning. She knew he was ensuring she was no social outcast—not allowing her to remain an object of pity. She held her head high and suddenly she found she truly no longer cared what any of them thought. Her freedom from all this was imminent and as a result she could actually enjoy it. There was no real pressure. She no longer had any *requirement* to perform. She wasn't going to be a princess for very much longer. She could just relax and, incredibly, she began to enjoy herself. She actually giggled at King Niko's mild joke. He too was kind and she softened towards him. No wonder he and Lucian were friends.

Afterwards, another man came over to her—a dashing captain from Niko's enormous entourage. He asked her to dance and she hid her reluctance and accepted. As they glided by the group around King Lucian she saw King Niko standing next to him now, watching her with a broad smile on his face. Lucian was also watching. But he looked as emotionless as ever.

'Princess Zara.' Another ultra-polite man from the party from Piri-nu asked her to dance. Then another.

Queen Maia seemed both awed and amused by the whole spectacle. She and King Niko frequently danced—always circling near to where Zara was dancing with yet more officers from Piri-nu. And in the times when they didn't dance, Zara chatted more and more easily with Maia, sipping cool drinks. She discovered Maia shared her sweet tooth so she delighted in telling her which of the delicate cakes were the best— especially the miniature caramel apple tarts. Zara was the only person King Niko danced with aside from his wife and Maia seemed particularly amused by the offers that Zara constantly received. Her dance card was very full indeed. It wasn't long before she didn't want it to be.

'Stop them, please,' Zara muttered in a laughing undertone to Maia. 'My feet are killing me.'

Maia giggled and took her arm. 'Then let's go find some more of those fancy cakes and hide.'

They sat in an alcove that afforded them some privacy while allowing them to watch proceedings. As Zara caught her breath she realised she wanted to savour this last experience. She wanted just a little more—to dance with Lucian. Just the once. She wanted a fairy-tale moment when the long-lost King returned and swept the rejected princess up and away.

But fairy-tales didn't happen in real life. Rejected princesses kept their chins up. They smiled. Even when their hearts were being crushed ever so slowly under the weight of unrequited, impossible affection.

Her only consolation was that Lucian danced with no one. Not once.

She caught his gaze once more from where she sat. Caught it, held it, melted inside. It was only when someone stepped from behind him that he startled and turned quickly away. She too turned, only to realise

Maia had been watching that wordless interaction. Maia had *seen*.

Zara felt a flush burnish her cheeks.

'What do you plan to do?' Maia asked softly.

About her future, right? Not about Lucian. There was nothing to be done about him.

'I want to go away,' she muttered.

'Not home?'

'No. I think I'm going to go to England.'

'You have friends there?'

Zara took a breath. 'No, but I need independence anyway.'

Maia had a gleam in her eye. 'You want to work?'

'While I get some formal qualifications.' She nodded. 'I didn't get the greatest education when I was younger.'

'Nor did I,' Maia said quietly. 'So I'm studying a couple of papers in Piri-nu.'

'You are?' Zara was surprised. 'That's great.'

'It's wonderful. I'm loving it.' Maia's smile widened. 'There are lots of courses. You shouldn't go to England. You should come to Piri-nu and train for whatever you want there. We have much better weather.' Enthusiasm made her speak faster. 'We could be study buddies.'

Zara giggled and shook her head. 'I couldn't—'

'Why not?' Maia suddenly took her wrist and pressed it tightly. 'I'm serious. If you need somewhere to go, come to *me*.' She glanced across the room to where Niko was conversing with Lucian and her voice dropped lower still. 'No one else needs to know. We do discretion really well there. I promise. I can help.'

Zara's heart thudded. Her gut told her Maia was genuine and lovely. 'Thank you. I might have to...'

She snatched a quick breath as she realised she might have a new plan that was even better. 'I'd pay you back.'

'I know you would.' Maia smiled. 'Just like Lucian.'

Zara's heart constricted.

'Take my private number now,' Maia insisted. 'Before Niko comes back and interferes.'

Zara's giggle was a touch watery, but she pulled herself together. 'Thank you.'

To her amazement, they all stayed at the ball almost until the very end.

'You've been so kind,' Zara said to Niko and Maia as they left the enormous room together. 'It was lovely to meet you both.'

'I wish you the very best, Princess.' Maia pulled her in for a quick hug and muttered into her ear, 'Let's see each other again very *soon*.'

It was very late but Zara opened the window to breathe in the cool winter air. She was horribly torn—partly relieved that the ball was over, yet despairing at the same time. She'd returned to a kind of public life, which meant she would have to leave here soon. It would look odd to all if she were to remain for much longer. She had to move forward with her life and now, thanks to Maia, she had an even better plan crystallising. But she was wide awake—not wanting the evening to end.

She heard the softest knock at her door. She'd known he would come. He stood silent, the heat in his gaze saying it all. She stepped back. In a heartbeat he was inside, quietly closing the door behind him. He scanned the room—assessing the windows. The exits. Checking security, as always. And, as always, she checked him. In his dark suit with the gold detail he looked suave and regal, but still dangerous and edgy. She knew he must be nearing exhaustion.

'You made it through the entire evening.' He spoke bluntly.

'I survived it, yes.' She put a hand on the back of the sofa, her legs weak at the sight of him.

'You didn't enjoy it?' he challenged huskily. 'That wasn't your laughter I heard across the ballroom?'

'It was for show.'

'Not entirely.' He walked towards her. 'I think you enjoyed it.'

Well, how could she not enjoy such an evening in a venue so stunning and the food so sublime? And most of the people—the ones she'd mingled with—had been courteous and kind. It had been a taste of the absolute privilege someone in her position *could* have.

'Maybe it wasn't so bad,' she admitted. 'King Niko and Queen Maia are lovely. And I liked the dancing.' She was surprised when he stiffened. 'Did you enjoy it?'

'Did I enjoy watching you look so beautiful as you danced with other men?' he muttered slowly.

'Well, that's your fault for ordering them all to dance with me,' she said softly, because she was sure that was what he'd done. 'I would have been happy to remain a social outcast. My feet are killing me.'

But he still didn't smile. 'I didn't order anyone to dance with you. I think that was Niko amusing himself at my expense.' His gaze heavy-lidded, he studied her mouth. 'He saw how furious I was when he first danced with you. I was jealous of my best friend. A man I know to be utterly in love with his wife.'

Oh, he was in a dangerous mood. Zara's heart thudded.

His glittering gaze skittered lower, sweeping over her silk gown. 'Will you have trouble getting out of your dress tonight?'

She stilled. 'I don't think I can manage the buttons.'

'I think you'd better or I'll end up shredding yet another of your dresses.'

A firestorm cascaded over her. She lifted shaking fingers and unfastened the first button. Then the next. Then the next.

He watched, utterly motionless, for a moment, only to suddenly shoot her a devastating smile. 'You prefer that I don't wear a jacket, right?'

She couldn't answer as he undid his buttons. And she forgot to finish unfastening her dress. Because he wasn't as butter-fingered as she and in the next moment he stood bare-chested before her. Her pulse quickened. So did her breathing. Because he didn't stop at the jacket and shirt. He toed off his shoes and unfastened the top button of his formal trousers—then somehow slid the zip down despite that bulge.

'You want me, Zara?' he asked huskily when he finally stood before her, fully naked. He was huge all over—tall, broad-shouldered, those large muscles rippling and his massive erection rigid. 'Because I want you.'

She was so relieved her knees went weak. He laughed throatily and caught her, sliding her to the floor, pushing the loosened silk from her body in seconds.

'Kiss me,' she begged.

'I intend to,' he growled. 'I'm going to do everything I've been dreaming of doing all damned night.'

He didn't just kiss her. He consumed her. Everywhere.

'Spread wider.' He pushed her thighs apart with his powerful hands and groaned. 'All mine.' He bent and feasted upon her. 'Only mine.'

'Yes.' She gasped at the rough swipe of his tongue and the silken soft brush of his lips.

'I can't get enough of you, Zara.' His grip on her tightened. 'I need this.'

'So do— *Oh, yes!*' She arched, her eyes almost rolling backwards as the decadent pleasure he gave overwhelmed her. She convulsed uncontrollably, lost in the throes of an orgasm so intense she barely remained conscious through it.

But he stroked her gently, keeping her with him, making her tumble deeper and deeper—because her want for him was endless.

'Zara…' He roused her again with the sexiest whisper. 'It's time for us to dance.'

The sexual smugness in his eyes as he reared above her made her even hotter. But he rose to his feet.

'Please,' she muttered almost inaudibly as he gazed down at her. 'Lucian—'

'We haven't made it to the bed,' he teased.

'I don't care.' She shivered greedily. 'Don't make me wait any longer.'

His body tensed. With a swift move that emphasised his jaw-dropping strength, he stepped between her legs and scooped her up. She immediately wrapped her legs around his hips, moaning at the sensation of having him hold her so completely. He was her iced-up man mountain, but he had a volcano inside him and when he erupted he bathed her in his searing vitality. She adored it when he let himself go like this. He planted his feet wide, anchoring them there in the centre of the room. His arousal pressed against her core. She pressed her hips closer to him as best she could. His gaze smouldered but she was ecstatic. She smiled right at him. He hissed and she saw the sexual restraint in him snap.

'I'm sorry I made you wait.' He slid her onto him in a slick, strong move.

She cried out in relief, in ecstasy, in raw, desperate need. He was so big and he held nothing back and it was *everything*.

'This is what you wanted?' he growled.

'Yes. More. Now.'

It was searingly physical and she relished it. As did he. He wrapped one arm around her hips, his other up her back, his hand spread to support her head. He impaled her onto him, over and over. They were both slick and hot. Both fiery and physical. He balanced her with shattering ease—it was entirely his strength keeping them upright, his strength sealing them together.

He grunted in feral appreciation of his complete domination of her, releasing gusts of hot air that teased her breasts as he thrust into her again and again. She clamped on him the only way she could—where he'd pushed in, gripping hard to lock him, fighting with her hands too—greedily grabbing his slick, strong muscles. He swore then, lifted his head and pulled her to meet his mouth. She moaned as he took her there too. He relentlessly drove deeper and deeper, claiming— *caressing*—her with everything he had.

She would never let him go. *Never*. She wrapped

herself even more tightly around him—clinging with every ounce of strength she had. Her body could stand the sensations only for so long. Every muscle screamed in sexual tension as he nailed her to him until she tore her lips free, her head falling back as a high-pitched, keening scream of release was ripped from her.

As she collapsed onto his shoulder she heard his shout echoing within her. She barely had any strength left to cling to him. But somehow he could still move. He carried her to the bedroom and carefully put her down on the bed. She needed more strength to pull him down to the bed with her, but she was too spent and he was too swift. He pulled free. Barely conscious, she whimpered at the loss of contact. She'd wanted to stay like that with him—not just entwined, but locked together. She wanted that always. But that wasn't what Lucian wanted. It wasn't *ever* what he would want. So, for all the bliss she felt, one corner of her heart broke as he pressed a too-gentle kiss to her cheek and whispered, 'Sleep.'

CHAPTER THIRTEEN

ZARA BARELY SAW Lucian the next day. There was nothing new in that except a melancholy swept over her, a sensation that was at odds with how she'd thought she'd feel. She'd thought she'd be relieved—that she'd cleared that challenging hurdle of the public appearance at the ball and her future would now be free of such things. But she'd actually enjoyed the evening more than she'd ever imagined she would. She'd enjoyed the conclusion of the night more than anything.

While most of the dignitaries had now left, the city was still in party mode. To have arranged something on this level in such a short time was an incredible feat and demonstrated just how completely—and quickly— Lucian had assumed control of the Crown. And how happy the country was to have him back.

She deliberately didn't check the papers. The media could be so fickle—positive one moment, shredding the next, so she knew it wouldn't serve her well. She would keep calm and carry on and quietly make her plans for a private, quiet life. She'd messaged Maia just to double-check she'd meant her offer of help. Maia's reply had been immediate. Zara knew she had her path now. Except there was that twist of yearning inside.

That night there was a dinner for the few dignitaries who'd remained for the extra day. She didn't attend. She hid in the private wing. But she saw him on his way to the banquet hall—clad in another fine woven suit. She stopped as he passed her in the corridor. She saw the exhaustion at the back of his eyes and could feel the strain emanating from him.

This was a man who'd survived a lot—who'd deliberately put himself into punishing, dangerous, demanding situations while working for Niko to strengthen his endurance and resilience—both physical and mental. But she knew his new life here was taking its toll. This was emotional. This was his home. Where he'd been born and raised and his parents had died. Where he'd been most vulnerable. Returning to face all this alone was challenging for him. He had so many memories tangled with contrary emotions. It exhausted her just to think about it, but he was the one *living* it. She knew he had much to do, but there had to come a point where he couldn't go on without decent rest. This constant hyper-alert state—seeking—*expecting*—danger all the time had to be punishing.

'Why aren't you coming to dinner?' he demanded in a low voice.

'Why do you think?' She shook her head at him. But her heart smote and she leaned a little closer. 'You can't go on like this. You're barely sleeping.'

His eyes flared. 'I have a job to do.'

'You can't do it properly without proper rest.'

He shot her a withering glance.

'Oh, please. As if you're not human?' she jeered. 'I know you're *very* human.'

There was a flicker in his eyes but he said nothing more as he walked past her.

It hurt. And it made her angry. He'd said nothing about the previous night. She knew there could be nothing more between them, but that restlessness was brewing again. So powerful, so complete. She was beginning to fear that the ache she felt for him was going to be unending.

So she stayed awake. She heard the bang and ripple of fading fireworks and knew those last guests would retire to bed soon. She knew which was his room. He'd taken the one only a few doors down from hers.

It was very late when she knocked on the door.

He said nothing when he opened it and saw her. But he reached for her wrist and hauled her inside. The suite was smaller than her own. Darker and spartan in its decor. It suited him. But she didn't linger to admire the furnishings. She walked directly to the bedroom.

'What are you doing?' he muttered as he followed her.

'You get to come to my room and take what you want, when you want. Why can't I do the same?'

'I thought I came to your room and gave you what *you* wanted.'

The challenge rippled through her. 'Okay then, what do you want from me?'

He stared at her and she just knew he was battling his self-control, overworked as it was.

She cocked her head and shot him a smile. 'My worst?'

With a groan he capitulated. 'Zara…'

The smile on his face then was so charmingly boyish and devilish it smote her heart. For a second the tortured, burdened man was gone and only humour and heat remained. She wanted to see *him* flushed and sated. She pushed him onto the bed. To her surprise, he actually fell backwards. She smothered a giggle as she knelt astride him. But then her smile faded—she wanted to touch him. To *give* to him.

She caressed the scar, it was a tough cord of gnarled skin, breaking the perfection of his eyebrow. And then she kissed him. His arms lifted—urging her closer. Too quickly. She pulled free and laughed again, before teasing him every way she could think of. Letting instinct—imagination…sheer curiosity—guide her. She swept her hand over his chest—tracing the tattoo, then the scar from the skating accident, the one that had helped identify him to the world. The other scars, the stories she didn't yet know. She wanted to know. Everything. And he lay back and let her—until he was shaking and incoherent and straining in that sweet torture.

'Lucian,' she breathed and bent to him again.

He roared his release and she swallowed the salty heat of him, stretching her hands wide to soothe his shudders, then licked her way back up his body.

'Pleased with yourself?' He held her above him.

She smiled. Then felt him move beneath her. Desire coloured her vision as he took his turn—his time— in teasing her. It was only moments until she couldn't stand any more. She moved quickly to mount him, grinding in absolute, fierce abandonment. Riding him was such pleasure. She gazed into his eyes and moaned as his devilish fingers teased, giving her the slightest of nudges to topple her over the edge.

'Zara.' He pulled her down to rest on him. 'Zara, Zara, Zara…'

His arms were so heavy, trapping her to him. This was what she'd wanted. What she'd ached for all this time. To be held by him—for them to be curled together in a tangle that *couldn't* be undone. With both of *them* undone. Able to rest at last.

Finally, he sank into sleep.

Hours later, Zara paced in the small lounge, silently biting her nails. Finally, she heard stirring from the room next door. A mutter. Then the thud of heavy footsteps.

'What time is it?' Lucian appeared in the doorway, naked save for a towel. He stared at the clock in horror. 'I slept for *nine hours*! I—'

'Clearly needed it.' She held her ground, hiding her knotted fingers behind her back.

His jaw dropped. 'What did you do? Surely Victor knocked?'

'I sent him away.'

'You *what*?' He looked astonished. Then irate.

'You needed sleep. I don't think you've slept for longer than a ninety-minute stretch in days.'

'You had no right.'

'No, but I did it anyway and I'm not sorry.'

'I have people to meet. I have a *country* that I owe—'

'You don't need to feel guilty about what happened.'

'I don't need you to mother me,' he snarled.

'Don't be reductive. I know perfectly well I'm not your mother. But I *am* your friend.'

'No—' he turned cold '—you're not my friend.'

'Suck it up, Lucian,' she flung back, instantly wounded. 'You're not invincible. You look so much better for it.'

That threw him. 'I look better?'

'You're not a machine, you know. You're human. With basic needs.'

'Needs?' he echoed and advanced on her.

She'd not seen him like this, his jaw stubbled, his hair slightly in tufts. Why had she ever thought those eyes of his were cold? But she backed up a pace because now he was looking feral.

'I thought you didn't want to be late for your meeting.'

'I'm so bloody late it barely matters now. What does matter is that I remind you who's in charge around here.'

She was suddenly as angry. With him for being angry. With herself for caring when it was so clear he didn't want her to. And how could he be so *useless* in caring for himself while at the same time demanding he meet impossibly perfect standards?

'Would that be you—lord and master?' she snapped. 'The great King himself. You want me on my knees?'

Yes, it was provocative. Deliberate. Dangerous. But she was alight with adrenalin.

'That's a very good idea,' he snapped.

Electricity charged the atmosphere. She wasn't afraid of the seething emotion. It was welcome. With a furious lift of her chin, she lowered first to one knee then the other and leaned back slightly to gaze all the way up to his fiery eyes.

'Drop the towel,' she said.

He froze.

'Drop the towel, Lucian.'

He was hard, proud, fierce. But the very last thing he was right now was in charge.

'Zara—'

She tugged the towel and took him in hand. Quite happy to hold him firmly. Quite happy to revel in the desperation of his gasp. She fluttered her fingers and then held him firm, while teasing the very tip of him with her tongue. Entirely on instinct. Entirely with feverish delight. And as her pleasure rose she moved restlessly, more rapidly, until she felt the vibrations in his muscles and heard the savage edge to his growl of frustration and need. She saw the clenched fists at his sides as he held back. She didn't want him to hold back. Ever. So she pressed closer still. Gripped harder. Rubbed harder. Sucked harder.

His hands thrust in her hair and his hips bucked wildly before he pulled away from her and snarled, '*Stop*.'

She stilled, panting, aching with emptiness.

'*All fours*.'

She looked into his expression and heat swamped her. Control lost to him again. But she gave it so willingly. The truth was *neither* of them were in control now. He had such need for her—for this at least. He dropped to his knees too, behind her. His hands slid, his fingers discovered her slick heat. And then his mouth.

She buckled, bending her head to the ground on a sob of ecstasy at how hot this was between them. Nothing but desire. No shame. No power game. Not any more. This was raw—as it always was because this emotion couldn't be contained and it was everything. It was rough but passionately so—not violent. Never that. The intensity with which he caressed her was stunning, as if he were desperate to drive her to that edge right with him. Reaching forward, he covered her widespread hand with his—laced then locked his fingers through hers. His chest was pressed flat along her back. He gripped her tightly, stopping her from being shunted away by his own force. And he didn't hold back. He pounded—deeper, harder, hotter. Owning her. Claiming her until she felt branded as his from the inside out. It was as if he couldn't get deep enough, close enough. As if it were a battle for his very survival—to be with her. It was the most animal of couplings. It would have been brutal if it weren't so beautiful. If there weren't such *feelings*. Desperation. Desire. Domination—yes. All lust—so close to love.

'Zara!' he growled. '*Zara!*'

But he pulled out and spun her over and suddenly was back, right back with her. In her. Only now he was gazing into her eyes and in his she saw that wild emotion. Such devastation. And his hold on her tightened even more as she shook apart and his big body finally quaked too. Until he collapsed over her. Utterly spent.

Such swift pleasure. Such abandonment. Such chaos. She closed her eyes. He was pinning her, but she was already his prisoner—shackled by the unbearable delight he gave.

The silence in the room was heavy, punctuated only by their jerky breathing. But as their rough gasps eased the atmosphere only seemed to sharpen.

'I am too heavy. I apologise.' He didn't even look her in the eyes. 'I had better get to that meeting.'

He took the towel and left the room. Left her there, all but catatonic on the floor. Shattered.

CHAPTER FOURTEEN

LUCIAN WAS FURIOUS with himself. He'd just exhibited a total loss of control. Again. He'd given in to an absolute emotional response. Again. He felt like a bastard. He'd been rude to her. He'd left her on the *floor*. What kind of human was he? He never should have touched her, never taken everything he wanted. Solace. Pleasure. So selfishly.

It was worsening. Trying to be near her—but not having her—simply caused carnage because, in the end, he lost control. Repeatedly.

He had no recollection of her leaving his bed this morning. Or of anyone knocking on his door. How could he not have woken? He couldn't remember the last time he'd slept as deeply or as soundly. But apparently every one of his senses had been dead to the world this morning. It was shockingly unacceptable—not only because of the risk to his personal safety but because he'd forgotten everything outside of that bedroom. He'd indulged in pure, physical comfort and neglected his work completely. *That* was not good enough.

He struggled to concentrate now. Also not good

enough. His country deserved better. Wasn't that why he'd returned?

He'd been determined to step up to the plate. To be the King his people deserved. And he'd known, hadn't he, that this needed his complete and undivided attention. Because when his personal desires were released, his performance dipped. Emotional distraction was utterly destructive.

But, given his failure, the only thing he could think was to switch his plan entirely. Ending this was apparently impossible, but if he could *tame* his own distraction then maybe he'd be better. The fact was they were drawn to each other. Their chemistry *refused* to be denied. So they shouldn't try. Maybe it was that denial that made it worse. So perhaps it needed its own bottle—to be contained and allowed out only at the *appropriate* time. He needed to strategically regain control of this situation. And he knew just how to do it.

'Zara.' He walked into the library with a tray in his hands. An offering. Caramel apple tart and tea.

She realised this was his wordless way of trying to make amends. She didn't want to accept wordless any more. That he'd brought it distressed her even more. Because he *almost* cared enough. He was courteous. Kind. Attentive even. Certainly passionate. But there it ended.

She watched him warily. 'I've written up a list of responses. The books are sorted. My work is done.'

He set the tray down and took the seat opposite, as he always did.

'I want you to marry me.'

Her heart stopped and it took her two tries to get her immediate answer out. 'We've been through this already.'

'I won't take no for an answer this time.'

She stared at him across the table. Trying to keep calm internally. Failing.

'Why?'

'It makes sense. It's the simplest, most effective solution.'

'To what problem?'

'To several problems.' He leaned towards her. 'You were right. I need an heir of my own and perhaps it needn't be in a decade after all. It would be efficient if I married you now.'

'Efficient? Because I'm already installed in the palace? Because I've already been vetted?'

His nostrils thinned. 'You're better at it than you give yourself credit for. You charm anyone you meet. You know what you're doing. You were beautiful at the ball.'

'Are you saying I could pass as a queen?'

He'd effectively listed some of Garth's reasons. She understood duty. She would be docile. A good enough clothes horse.

'Are there any *personal* reasons why you think this is a good idea?' She barely kept her tone cordial.

'I trust Victor, but I think, after this morning, everyone will know there's something between us. This will leak, Zara. Our marriage will protect you from those complications.'

'Because my reputation needs protecting? Didn't you once ask what century this is?' She glared at him. 'Anything else?'

A muscle in his jaw flexed. 'We're good together.'

'Do you mean in bed? Because we haven't often actually *made* it to a bed.'

Once, in fact. His bed. Where they'd both slept like newborns. But the afterglow this time was now more like an after *burn*. It wasn't the love bites on her breasts or the grazes on her inner thighs from his stubbled jaw this morning causing the sting.

We're not friends.

It hurt. Deeply. He wanted her. He liked her. Respected her even. He'd been kind. He wanted her physically. But he *didn't* love her. And she knew he'd fight to keep part of himself separate from her. Always. His heart was out of bounds to everyone.

'Anything else?' she prompted again.

'You don't have anywhere else to go. You have no real plan, Zara.'

Not true, actually. Not any more. But she kept that to herself for now. Because he still wasn't offering the reason she really wanted.

'You were angry with me this morning,' she said. 'I overstepped your mark. What if I overstep it again?'

'I was taken by surprise. If we're married, there won't be the need for secrecy. Nor will there be any uncertainty—'

'You mean you'd know I would be in your bed every night,' she said.

He nodded.

'You want stability and certainty,' she clarified.

In *every* element of his life. She *could* be a convenient wife to him. Useful. Suitable. And perhaps she could support him in the limited ways he could accept. And the thing was, she would have accepted his proposal only weeks ago. It was the kind of marriage she'd thought she would get with Anders. But not now. She wanted more. She wanted unconditional, absolute love. And she wanted it from him. *Only* him.

But *he* didn't want that. Not with her or anyone.

'There's another problem that you haven't factored in,' she said.

'Oh?' He waited.

She was shaking inside. 'You won't like it.'

He waited but she felt horribly tight in the throat.

'I don't usually have to prise information from you, Zara.' He regarded her steadily with those pale blue eyes. 'You can tell me anything.'

'I've fallen in love with you,' she whispered. 'I have. Fallen in love. I realise this wasn't supposed to happen.' Her heart skipped as she watched him. 'And I know it's not what you want in this proposal of yours.'

There was no reaction. None. He was still as stone.

'So I hope you'll understand that it's best that I say no. It's also best that I leave now,' she muttered, quickly standing up.

'Are you going to throw that pertinent fact out and then run away?'

'Don't.' She paused, two steps from the table. 'I'll get angry.'

'Go on then.' He stood too. 'Get angry.'

Fury flared. 'I just told you I'm in love with you and you say nothing, other than to demand *more* from me? When you give me *nothing* at all in response.'

'Because there's nothing I can say to that.'

'Not even a thank you? Not even that you appreciate my honesty?' She was suddenly incandescent. 'Because you obviously can't reciprocate.'

'We're…' He dragged in a breath. 'We're *friends*.'

For a man determined to remain so distant, the acknowledgement of any kind of emotion should be a win, she supposed painfully. But it wasn't.

'Are we? Wow. I thought we were only lovers. Even then barely. I'm merely an uninvited guest who you sometimes have sex with.'

He stared at her rigidly.

'But that you care a little is more than I ever should have expected.'

'From me?'

'*For* me.' She shook her head.

He blanched and took a step towards her. 'Why can't this be enough for you? Why risk…?' He breathed out. 'This is good. This *is*.'

A man who could hardly stand her to stay the whole night with him?

Lucian was everything, except for that block of ice in his heart. That part of him she could never touch. That part he didn't ever want to give her. That part he'd locked away for good.

'You disappeared for the best part of a decade,' she said. 'I'm going to do the same. I'm going to Piri-nu.'

For a full minute he was silent. 'Disappearing isn't all it's made out to be, Zara,' he gritted. 'It's not for you.'

'You don't think I can handle it?'

'Your skin will burn.'

'I'll use sun lotion and cover up.'

'You'll still be too hot.'

'I'll get used to it.'

'You'll miss the snow.'

'I'll get used to missing *many* things. People adjust to new circumstances when they have no choice.'

'It won't be enough.'

'Friends and a warm welcome won't be enough?' she challenged. 'It was for you. Why not me?' She was so hurt. 'I want to go somewhere new. Somewhere where I don't have to be a princess. Where I don't have to be a disappointment and where I don't have to be *disappointed*.'

'You should have more.'

'Then *offer me more*,' she snapped back.

He froze.

'You don't want to,' she said quietly. 'You're *scared*. You're clinging to an impossible ideal of self-control and sacrifice as if it can somehow make you worthy and keep you *safe*. I don't blame you. I can't imagine the pain you've endured. But I can understand the loneliness.' She lifted her head. 'It shouldn't be like that for always. You have too much to give.'

'There's nothing.' He was barely audible.

'Not true.'

'There's nothing I *want* to give.'

And there it was.

'You don't *want* anyone to truly care about you,' she said. 'Because you don't care about yourself.'

He *hated* himself. It wasn't Anders who was his real enemy at all.

'You can carry the Crown, Lucian, but to carry someone's heart… To accept their love? That's impossible for you. You're so guilt-ridden you struggle to accept the respect of your subjects. You can hardly accept tenderness from me. Sex, yes. But an act of caring—of compassion?' She shook her head. 'This is totally the wrong time for you. Totally. You're busy. And you don't want this. And I'm so very sorry for you.'

'So it's pity not love you feel. I thought you were brave,' he snarled. 'Ready to take on the world as you want it.'

'That's exactly what I am doing,' she said. 'I want independence but I don't believe that equates to emotional isolation the way you do. To me they're two very different things. We would want different things in our marriage.'

'What do you think I would want?'

'Stability, security. Everything you've said. Perhaps to protect me, also. Because you pity me and you take on guilt even when you're not responsible. Because we're good in bed together. At least for now. You think you can keep yourself safe for ever. But you can't. It's impossible. You can't even accept a little help.'

He'd just offered her what she desperately wanted and it was the worst feeling ever because it wasn't for the *reasons* she needed.

'I *can* accept help till I get on my feet,' she said proudly. 'I know I can't do everything all on my own, all of the time. You can't either. But you won't admit that. You won't even see it.'

'Don't think you need to fix me.'

'Neither of us need to be *fixed*,' she snapped. 'But you need to *forgive* yourself. You need to heal. I can't do it for you. And you *can't* know what you really want until you've processed that.'

'And how do you know what you really want?' he jeered.

'By knowing what I *don't* want. And I don't want this.' She dragged in a painful breath. 'I actually do need you to be my friend, Lucian. I need you to put *my* wellbeing ahead of your own temporary desires,' she said. 'I know you don't want to hurt me. I know you've *never* wanted to hurt me. And this would.'

'I am not as honourable as you seem to think.' His control slipped. '*This* is not what *I* want, Zara.'

'Well, we don't always get what we want. Not even kings.' She finally lost it. 'Find someone as heartless as yourself,' she said. 'Because that's not me.'

'Zara—'

'I'm being *honest*. Which is more than you can seem to be,' she flared at him. 'I'm in love with you. And I know you feel something for me too. But you can't even admit what that is, let alone embrace it. If it's just lust, that's fine, Lucian. But at least admit it. And if it's lust it will fade. Signing up to a lifetime commitment right now is *madness*. Especially when the truth is you want to be alone. You've made that very clear. I'm not going to live where I'm not loved—I need to be loved, just for myself. My family didn't love me enough like that.'

'You happily accepted a similar offer from Anders only weeks ago, yet somehow I am *worse* than—'

'And I was *wrong* about him. And thank you for stopping it. You've opened my eyes in many ways, Lucian. And now I know that for me to accept *your* proposal is even more wrong. It's *so* different. Knowing you don't feel the same would only destroy me.'

He became a statue once more. 'I do not want to see you destroyed. I'm sorry you feel that is what would happen if you were to accept my proposal,' he said stiffly. 'Piri-nu is a place of sanctuary. I will make the arrangements.'

'How long will that take?'

'You can leave as soon as you would like.'

'I'm already packed.'

'Then I'll get onto it immediately.'

He was true to his word. Zara had been standing, shell-shocked, in her room for only twenty minutes before there was a peremptory knock on her door.

Lucian stood there, the aviator sunglasses back on. 'You'll go by helicopter to a private runway in Austria. An unmarked jet will be there. It will take you direct to Piri-nu.'

He was silent as he carried her bag to the helipad. She didn't know what she'd wanted. What she'd hoped for. He was utterly cold and emotionless. Only that wasn't true. That wasn't the Lucian she knew. *Intimately.*

He faced her, all ice. 'I've used you. Abominably. I apologise. I cannot make amends. I can only apologise.'

She stared at him sadly. 'Are you not angry right now, Lucian?' Because she was furious.

He barely hesitated. 'I'm always angry, Zara.'

Yeah, and he made her even angrier. He still couldn't be vulnerable—or honest.

She stepped right up to him. 'Anger is an expression of *hurt*. Of *other* feelings that have been wounded. Because *you* feel deeply and you feel *lots* of things. Including love. You're just trying far too hard not to.'

He was stuck trying to protect himself—so he wasn't really living at all.

'*I* chose to come here. I chose to stay. I chose to have this affair with you.' She straightened proudly even as her voice shook. 'And now I choose to end it. That's where you can't stand in my way.' But the hurt leaked out in stinging tears that coursed down her cheeks. 'Stay suffering, Lucian. Stay drowning in your unnecessary guilt.' She dragged in a hiccupping breath. 'You know we could have had *everything* but you're too scared.'

He took a half-step nearer before stopping himself. 'Please don't cry, Zara.'

'You might like to mask every emotion,' she cried. 'Pretend like you feel nothing. But I'm not going to. It won't make it go away. It won't just disappear. Loving people and losing them hurts, Lucian. Like this is for me, right now. And not even you can deny it.'

CHAPTER FIFTEEN

PIRI-NU WAS EVERY bit as hot as Lucian had warned.
Every bit as beautiful. Gold-ringed emerald islands,
sapphire waters, the widest of skies. It was a paradise,
where anything would be possible.

'The air-conditioning is fantastic, isn't it?' Maia
smiled as she joined Zara in the beautiful lounge a
week after her departure from Monrayne.

'I'll acclimatise.'

'Give it time. It's a big adjustment.'

The croissant Zara had selected for lunch was the
lightest, most buttery pastry she'd ever eaten, but she
couldn't finish it. Her appetite—so endless back in
Monrayne—was deadened here. The heat, she supposed. Heat and heartache. She would get used to both.
She would cope. Ultimately, she would thrive.

She finally had the freedom she'd wanted. No title.
No expectations. No need to seek impossible approval.
Not from her family. Not from Lucian either. She would
be herself and she would be okay.

'You and Niko have been so kind.' She gestured towards the campus prospectuses Maia had gathered for
her. 'I'm excited to work through these.'

'I'm glad.' But Maia's expression turned cautious as

she sat beside Zara. 'Are you okay, though?' she asked quietly. 'Have you been in touch with Lucian?'

Zara's heart skidded. Maia hadn't asked about him until now.

'No.'

Maia nodded but couldn't quite hide her curiosity. 'I had the feeling you were close...'

Zara shook her head. 'Apparently we're *friends*,' she muttered.

But they really weren't.

Sympathy softened Maia's eyes. 'I had no idea of Lucian's past before Niko told me. It must be very complicated for him and he must have so much to deal with,' she said. 'I'm sorry if things haven't worked out the way that *you* wanted. Take the time you need to rest, here. Grieve. Then go on.'

Zara nodded, appreciating Maia's honesty and her restraint. She didn't attempt to make it better and offered no false reassurances. It was what it was. And it was over.

She'd contacted her parents, simply to let them know she was safe and well and hoped they were the same. A small part of her still wanted to please them—her inner child who craved their attention, love and approval. But the adult in her needed this chance to live her life fully and not settle for less.

She didn't try to contact Lucian. She needed a complete break to recover. Because she had been just that distraction—like a balm to help him get through a brutal time. She'd offered physical contact, amusement, maybe the smallest solace. But there wasn't depth to it. She'd overstepped the boundaries he'd tried to keep. Her fault for taking it so seriously and thinking she could get beneath the gnarled, scarred tissue protecting his heart. He didn't want her to do that. And that was fair enough. Who was she to demand more than what he was willing to give? Just as he shouldn't demand she take less than what she wanted too.

They wanted each other, liked each other even. But, ultimately, they wanted different things.

Lucian wished he'd refused Zara when she'd requested to leave just over a week ago. He could have been a demanding dictator but he'd helped her leave instead, making it as swift as possible. Not because he'd been determined to do the right thing but because it was what she'd needed from him. Because he couldn't give her what she'd said she *wanted*.

Because he couldn't believe what she'd said she felt.

Because he couldn't have stood to hear her say it ever again.

He could not be the man for her. He had to be King more than man. Duty had to supersede the personal. What was best for her would never be him—not now, not even in that damned decade he'd banked on. How badly he'd just hurt her proved it, right?

'Zara has settled in well. Maia's enjoying her company very much. They've been spending a lot of time together.'

He really didn't want to listen to Niko right now but he couldn't slam the phone down on his friend.

'That's great,' he said mechanically.

There was a silence then a growl from Niko. 'I know I always beat you in calculus but I didn't realise you were actually *this* unintelligent,' he said.

'You never beat me in calculus. I helped you.'

'That's not how I remember it,' Niko shot back blithely. 'But, either way, you need to sort your head, Lucian.'

'Because…?'

'You know why,' Niko said. 'You've just let the best thing to hit your life leave.'

Lucian gave up any pretence of ignorance. 'What has she told you?'

'Nothing. It was obvious at the ball, Lucian. You couldn't take your eyes off her.'

Yeah, that was part of the problem.

'You know you were going through the motions for years here on Piri-nu. Working hard, building strength, amassing resources, silently seething, barely existing… but you actually smiled when you mentioned her to me when I arrived. Did you even know you did that?'

Lucian closed his eyes. She'd always made him smile.

'It's the most alive I've seen you in *years*,' Niko added brutally. 'Don't sink back into that numb state now—'

'Niko—'

'No, I don't want to hear whatever the excuse is.' Niko spoke over him. 'I know there are issues. We all have them. You damn well know I do. That Maia does. But you also know I'm better when I'm alongside her. Same thing, brother. You'll handle everything better with Zara beside you. So will she. That's how it works.'

'I'm not what she needs—'

'Are you sure about that?' Niko growled. 'Because she looked mighty alive to me that night too. Less so now.'

Lucian tensed. 'You said she was settling in well.'

Niko paused. 'You can't deny you care about her.'

'That isn't the point.'

'Isn't it? Because I think you know she cares about you. And I think that scares you so much you've sent her away.'

Damn Niko. Lucian needed him to back off.

'If the stuff holding you back is heavy, then get help to sort it,' Niko said more gently. 'You can't let the past stop you from being happy—not now you have this chance in front of you. Don't stall out. Don't waste any more *time*, Lucian. It's too precious. I never understood that before...'

Lucian knew Niko was thinking of his wife and his unborn child. He knew how his friend had fought to have them.

'Trust in this,' Niko continued after a beat. 'Let that old stuff go and *trust*. I promise you it'll be worth it.'

Lucian's thoughts inexorably turned back to Zara. To those moments when he'd held her and she'd held him. To that night when he'd slept more peacefully than ever. He'd been safe in her arms and she'd tried to tell him he always would be.

'What's she doing now?' he asked quietly.

'No, I'm not going to be your spy. If you want to know how she is then come and see her for yourself.'

Niko rang off. Lucian gritted his teeth, that old anger flaring. But it wasn't anger. Zara been right about that too. She'd called anger an expression of hurt—of betrayed trust, bruised love, burning regret. So many feelings that he'd hated but couldn't stop. They surged in him now and so many others tumbled in too. He couldn't stand it. Niko was right. He needed help to sort it. Because he couldn't stay as he was—not even stalled but submerged in an emotional mess that he couldn't process.

But he needed to. Wanted to. Now.

Lucian stood at the window and looked out at his city. One time at dinner Zara had described it as 'snow-globe-perfect'. But a snow globe needed a good shake to bring its vibrant beauty forth. Apparently, Lucian needed more than one good shake. He'd needed to hear the plain truth from both Zara and Niko.

The palace was as lifeless as a tomb—mirroring how he felt inside. He hated the emptiness. Hated how he ached inside and out as he acknowledged the truth. He'd been more awfully selfish than ever—asking everything of her and not offering the real truth about himself. He'd given her his body, sure. A place in his palace. But he'd not trusted her to tell her she had his battered heart.

And it was way past time that he did.

CHAPTER SIXTEEN

Zara checked that she was fully in the shade and then stretched out. She was acclimatising slowly to the temperature and at peak heat she needed to just relax with a book. Only she kept reading the same line over and over.

'Zara?'

Aviator sunglasses. Stubbled jaw. Massive muscles. He had that slightly on-edge aura about him. That element of danger.

Zara sat bolt upright. 'You shouldn't be here. You shouldn't have left Monrayne. It's too soon for you to be away for long.'

'No one knows I'm away and the jet is being refuelled as we speak.'

'You're going straight back?' Her heart lurched. 'How long are you planning to be on the ground?'

'As long as it takes to tell you some things face to face.'

He wanted to talk? Her wariness escalated.

'I guess you're lucky I'm here.' She stood. 'I could've been on a boat. Maia's been taking me around the islands but she was too tired today...'

She trailed off as she saw the glimmer of guilt on

Lucian's face. Of *knowledge*. Had Maia known he was coming? She had phoned Zara's suite this morning and insisted on making up for it by arranging for Zara to have a full spa treatment. She'd been so full of apologies Zara hadn't been able to refuse.

As a result, Zara had been pampered all day. That was why she was standing here now feeling like some glamorous nineteen-fifties movie starlet with her hair sleek, skin buffed, toenails painted and clad in a pretty silk dress that just brushed her mid-thigh. No one would ever guess she'd been crying her heart out upon waking every morning this last week.

'You look like you're enjoying it here,' he said.

Yes, Maia had conspired against her. But while she might have known Lucian was going to surprise her, she'd also ensured Zara was looking her absolute finest when she faced him. Which made Maia a *true* friend and ally.

'Very much,' she said. 'Niko and Maia have been wonderful to me. I understand why you chose to stay here.'

'You prefer it to Monrayne?'

'It's very different,' she answered noncommittally.

He took a breath and stepped closer. 'When I last left here I thought my future was pretty simple. I'd return to Monrayne, expose Anders, reclaim the throne and do the right thing for my country. I'd strive to be a good King. I would stay focused. Stay selfless. I even made a vow—to do nothing but that for the decade ahead. I promised, Zara. But it was an impossible task. Part of me remains greedy.'

Her heart splintered. 'Because you're a human, not a robot.'

He nodded. 'Right, because I tried to live without half of life's necessities. No rest. No recreation. No intimate relationship.'

He took off his glasses and she saw the emotion warming his eyes.

'You think those are necessities now?' she breathed.

He hesitated a moment. 'I've had a couple sessions with my old therapist because returning was harder to handle than I thought it would be. The panic attack. The sleeplessness...'

'Most people who'd been through what you've been through would be the same. You've lost a lot. But Lucian, I was just...' She cleared her throat. 'I was in the right place and I was convenient. That's all. You don't have to pretend that what happened between us meant anything more than that for you.'

His eyes flared. 'Zara—'

'I'm okay. I'm not destroyed—' she hurriedly interrupted him '—I've got through lots of tough things and I'll get through this. Maybe I just latched onto you too because you made me feel...wanted. Certainly not frigid around you, so thank you for that, I guess.'

'You thank me?' He stepped closer. 'Are you saying it wasn't as precious to you as you said only a few days ago?'

Her heart broke all over again. She couldn't lie to him. She adored him and right now she was both so happy and so sad she lost the power of speech.

'No?' He traced her face softly. 'You can't say that?'

She closed her eyes briefly. This wasn't fair.

'This is not a *convenience*, Zara,' he whispered. 'This is not a distraction. This isn't an alternate kind of comfort-eating through an emotional time. *You* are the emotion—all of them. *You* are the upheaval. You are *everything*. I walked into that damned cathedral, ready to slay the dragon from my past and I took one look at you and promptly forgot who I was and why I was there at all. *Everything* fell away and nothing but you mattered.'

'It was the dress,' she muttered. 'It was blinding. There were so many jewels all over it—'

'It wasn't the damned dress.' He laughed on a breath. 'You turned. Looked at me. You saw me. And I saw you. Here.' He pressed his hand on his heart but his eyes burned bluer with frustration even as his voice grew softer. 'But it was impossible. The *worst* timing. You were wounded by Anders, your family. And I was seeking not revenge, but *redemption*, just as you said. You were right in everything, Zara. I'm trying very hard not to mask my emotions any more. I want to be honest. I need you to believe me. To trust me.'

'Of course I trust you,' she muttered. 'You've always been honest with me—'

'No, I haven't. I lied to you, Zara. Lied by omission when I didn't tell you...'

She stilled. 'Didn't tell me what?'

'That I love being with you. That I love you talking incessantly to me. I love trying to make you laugh. I love it when we're just hanging out. Being with you makes me forget everything bad that ever happened. But the thing is I can't use you like that. You're not my therapy dog, remember? I want to be fully present, to be one hundred percent. For Monrayne, yes, but mostly for you. Can you be patient while I get there, Zara?'

'Are you asking me to wait for you?'

His lips twisted as he shook his head. 'Maybe a

better man would. But I waited a decade before taking the throne back from Anders and I'm not waiting a decade before sorting myself enough to be with you. I don't want to miss out on any more *time*. I want you *with* me to do that. I want you to come back with me right now. But I'm going to be working on things for a while. Could you tolerate being around while I do that, do you think?'

He wanted her with him. He wanted to be with her. Because he loved her. And he was still holding himself to overly exacting standards.

'I'm not exactly perfect and whole myself, you know,' she muttered. 'I get nervous in public. I can write, but put me in front of a crowd and I just want to vomit.' She paused. 'Except when I'm with you. I don't feel like throwing up then. I feel courageous around you. After all, I successfully blackmailed you…'

'You did.' He smiled.

'So I guess I used you a little too.'

'You can use me any time, anyhow, you like.'

Her heart raced. 'You want me—'

'Back. Now. Because I'm absolutely and utterly in love with you,' he said huskily.

She stared up at him and those tears filled her eyes.

'You can take time to think about it if you need and fly a bit later. If I'm rushing you—'

'Life with you will always be intense,' she whispered. 'You don't actually do life any other way.'

'I'm trying very hard to hold back now.'

'What would you do if you didn't hold back?'

'I'd pick you up, get you to the jet and take off before you could stop me.'

'And then?'

'Spend the rest of my days serving Monrayne and loving you. I want to do everything with you beside me. And I would never let you go again.'

'Then don't hold back, Lucian. Don't ever hold back with me again.' She launched herself into the arms of her mountain of a man. His ice had melted and the warmth of him was utterly intoxicating. He was big and strong and she just buried herself in his hold as he carried her to the waiting car. They didn't speak a word on the short drive. They were too busy kissing.

But as he led her up the stairs of the jet he smiled. 'What if I told you there's a caramel apple tart on board the jet?'

'Why didn't you say that first up?' she teased. 'We would have been in the air twenty minutes already.'

'Zara…' He laughed.

She'd been too busy crying to pay too much attention to the interior of the private plane the last time she'd flown in it and she was too busy drinking him in this time. The second the jet levelled out after take-off Lucian unfastened his belt and came to her.

But she held him at bay, the practicalities worrying her. 'You're going to smuggle me back into the palace, right? I'll just live there quietly and secretly for—'

'Ever? No way. You've lived like that almost all your life. Not happening. You're going to travel. You're going to study, you're going to manage whatever projects you want, save all Monrayne's old castles if you want—'

'It's going to be weird.'

'It's going to be fine. You just move in. We won't care what anyone has to say on it.'

'I can't just start living at the palace.'

'Why not? Cutting one side of your life out completely isn't healthy and it isn't sustainable. Trust me on that. You've never had the experience of living as an actual Royal. Give it a chance.' He tempted her with the most gorgeous smile. 'Be my date. Dance with me. I'll come see your parents with you. We'll travel together wherever. I want more balance. We'll take weekends. Summer holidays. We can come back here—' He broke off and drew breath. His lips twisted in apology. 'But no pressure for more than that. I've tried to get you to marry me twice recently and I'm not risking rejection again yet. You need time to make sure this is a life you want. Time where you're free to come and go and do whatever you want. Because there will be limitations if you choose to become my wife. I don't want you to miss out on experiencing your full freedom first. So I'm not going to propose again for a year. Three hundred and sixty-five days exactly. I promise. Will you give Monrayne and *me* that chance?'

She stared into his amazing eyes, knowing that there was no disentangling the man from his Crown. And that was as it should be.

'Of course I will.' Her heart thudded. 'Promise you won't ask anyone else in that time either.'

'What? Zara,' he admonished. 'Do you think any other woman would please me?' he said thickly. 'Do you think I want this with anyone else? Only you.' He claimed her intimately. 'Only you will ever do for me.'

Her mouth parted on a wordless sigh as he drew her even closer.

'I know you like that,' he muttered, watching the colour wash over her skin. 'I like it too.'

Pleasure flooded her swiftly. She was so happy, so

certain of him that she couldn't resist teasing him. 'It's just that I'm your first.'

'Rubbish.' He nuzzled her neck and laughed. 'You're the only one I've wanted like this. I was waiting. Not for the right moment but for the right person.'

So seductive. So true. For her too. But she couldn't help another smile as she swept her fingers down his sternum. 'I just thought you were hot.'

He narrowed his gaze and moved a little harder, deeper, faster. 'The bare chest?'

'You know I can't see past it,' she sighed.

He chuckled. 'That was my back-up plan in case you weren't willing to listen to me when I got to Piri-nu.'

'That and the caramel apple tart.' She laughed but she spread her palm over his old ice-skating scar and felt the strong thud of his heart. It grounded her in the searing heat between them. 'It's not just the chest,' she whispered.

'I know,' he whispered back. 'You love me.'

'I do.'

'Best thing ever. I'm sorry I pushed you away. Sorry I didn't know how to accept it. That I was too scared to answer honestly at the time.' He cupped her face. 'But I'm getting better at it. I love you too.'

He was brave and strong, loyal and honourable and *hers*. She'd never felt as happy as she did in that moment.

'Take me home, Lucian.'

Her body shook as he unleashed his absolute force on her.

'*Yes!*'

CHAPTER SEVENTEEN

Three hundred and sixty-four days later

LUCIAN WAS LATE to dinner.

Zara toyed with the cutlery. Silly nervous. Her brain refused to get off one track. Tomorrow would be a year to the day that he'd found her on Piri-nu and brought her back home to his palace in Monrayne. A year in which he'd promised he wouldn't propose to her. He hadn't said he *would* propose on this day of course, just that he wouldn't propose *before*. Which meant that he might not propose at all. Of course, there'd been nothing stopping her from asking him in all this time, except she'd thought that as he thought she needed time, perhaps *he* really needed time... To be certain that was. Because she already was. She had been from the start.

'Sorry.' He shot her an apologetic smile as he finally walked in. 'Back-to-back meetings. Both ran over.'

'It's okay.'

He'd been oddly preoccupied the last couple of weeks. He probably hadn't even remembered what date it was.

His coronation had occurred seven months after his return and two months before Anders was found at the bottom of a cliff in South America. Apparently he'd accidentally lost control of his motorcycle on a corner, but Lucian had suspicions that he'd crossed swords with career criminals and been chased down. It had been a sad end to an unhappy life. Garth had been fined and retired quietly into the countryside, his time in the palace now consigned to the history books.

But Lucian's reign had simply strengthened from its astonishing start, while Zara's residence in the palace had been accepted with a surprising lack of side-eye. Lucian had offered a short explanation that she was a friend, staying indefinitely. It hadn't taken the media, citizens and rest of the world that long to work out that she was a 'special' friend, given she accompanied him on every evening outing he attended. And any trips he took abroad. That she also went with him on his weekends away and on his summer retreat into the hills…

To *her* astonishment, it seemed they *approved* of her. They liked her honesty, her moments of awkwardness, her appreciation. And they loved the way *he* smiled when he was with her. That he'd stopped her from marrying someone else had been spun into a feted romance—as if it were a fairy-tale.

It wasn't. It was so much better than that. It was funnier, lovelier, hotter. He'd given her a life of luxury, taken her to amazing places she'd never imagined getting to see and introduced her to wonderful people. He'd also supported her as she undertook part-time study in the management and conservation of historic buildings—the part of her previous life that she'd actually loved. Plus she'd kept working on the palace correspondence—they worked on it together now. And with Zara's help he'd opened other parts of the palace to the public. But she liked being here with him in the older, private palace wing best. Working alongside him in the library. Dining with him here in their room. Being held by him in their bed.

'You're not hungry?' Lucian noticed her pushing the food around the plate.

She shrugged and jerked her chin towards his plate. 'You've not done much better.'

He smiled ruefully and pushed back his chair, stepping round to kiss her. Thoroughly.

'Do you know we've made love in every room in the palace, yet not in here,' he muttered. 'How has that happened?'

'We've always been distracted by caramel apple tart,' she murmured.

'Ah. Yes, that's very sweet, but not as sweet as you.' He released her with a groan. 'But we can't tonight because I've still got a million reports to wade through. I'm sorry.'

'And I have reports of my own to write,' she said, though it was going to be a struggle to concentrate. 'I'll do it in bed.'

'I'll join you as soon as I can.'

But a long time later he still hadn't made it up to their suite. She turned the light out yet couldn't sleep. Still nervous. She loved living with him. She would live here for the rest of her days just like this. But she wanted more. She wanted a family with him. She dreamed of the two of them having it *all* together.

'Zara?' She heard his voice in her dreams, husky and loving. 'Are you awake, darling?'

She stirred drowsily. 'What time is it?'

'Just past midnight.'

He sounded very serious and she came fully awake. 'Is something wrong?'

He lit the small lamp on the table and sat on her side of the bed. 'I wanted to keep my promise, but not for a second longer than I have to.'

'Your promise?'

There was the barest hesitation, an indrawn breath. 'Will you marry me, Zara?'

Tears instantly sprang to her eyes, but nothing could hold back her smile. Or her answer. 'You know I will.' Shamelessly joyous, she threw her arms around his neck and tugged him down to her. 'I thought you'd *never* ask again!'

His kiss was hotter than ever—lush and long—and it didn't matter that she was both laughing and crying.

'It's been a very long year biting that question back every bloody day,' he groaned. 'And these last weeks I've been going round the bend, trying to dream up the perfect way to propose. I thought about taking you to Piri-nu. About lighting up the sky with fireworks. I even tried to figure out when and how to bake the engagement ring into a caramel tart…' He shook his head. 'In the end I just couldn't wait.'

'And I'm so glad,' she breathed. 'This is perfect. I'm so glad you didn't wait a second longer. I was working up the courage to ask you—' She broke off and narrowed her gaze on him. 'What engagement ring?'

'Good thing you've stopped biting your nails.' He chuckled but her heart smote as she gazed at the ring he held for her.

It wasn't like any she'd seen before. Set in gold, this was a series of baguette cut sapphires, creating a kaleidoscopic effect. Like a hall of mirrors, the stones shifted from the deep blue stone in the centre to pale at the edges.

'I had it made specially,' he explained huskily. 'It hasn't belonged to anyone else. So there's no baggage or bad memories with it.'

'We can't always escape baggage,' she whispered.

'No. But perhaps we could put the baggage in a cupboard sometimes and unpack it slowly in those moments when we have the strength to bother.' He slid the ring down her finger. 'I don't want to be burdened by the past. By the expectations of others. I don't want that for you either. You'll wear all the family jewels, but this one is just for you from me.' He pointed to the central stone. 'It's the colour of your eyes.'

'And they run all the way down to the colour of yours,' she added, pointing to the palest stones at the edge. 'I love it.'

'Good,' he growled and pushed her back down on the bed. 'Because I love you.'

They were swift then. Whispering words of love and tenderness and relief. Then there were no words, only that delicious tension as sighs quickened and bodies heated.

'You know we'll have to get married in the cathedral,' he said, holding her close after.

'Oh?' She froze.

'But I was thinking we could do it at some ridiculously early hour when everyone else is asleep. If you're very lucky I might even go bare-chested.'

A wave of amusement washed over her.

'Half-naked nuptials?' She giggled and pressed her forehead against his chest. 'Lucian.'

'We can do whatever we want,' he said softly.

'We can*not*,' she said prosaically. 'But I will get into another wedding dress. I'll walk down a long, scary aisle in front of millions. Only for you.'

His arms tightened. 'Thank goodness. I thought I was going to have to kidnap you. But if you like we can have a private wedding ceremony as soon as possible, followed by a public blessing a little later, once the pageant has been organised. A compromise. What do you think?'

'Not having to walk up the aisle, terrified someone might *stop* it actually sounds really good to me,' she admitted.

'No one will be able to stop it,' he promised. 'Because we'll already be married.'

'That sounds perfect.' She smiled.

And it was.

CHAPTER EIGHTEEN

Four years after that

LUCIAN WATCHED IN amusement as Niko walked towards him—one child on his hip, another walking alongside him, holding his hand. Maia was a step in front, holding yet another toddler, while the last was in the arms of a nanny. An entourage of assistants followed.

'Wow.' Lucian removed his sunglasses and smiled broadly as he took in the spectacle. 'How was the flight?'

'Piece of cake.' Niko winked.

The good humour was so very typical of his larger-than-life friend.

'What else is a ten-hour journey with triplet toddlers and a five-year-old?' Lucian stepped forward to scoop up the nearest small person tottering rather unevenly on the frosty path.

'I always forget how cold your country is, Pax.' Niko shivered and wrapped his spare arm around his wife. 'But it's lovely to see your smile.' He cocked his head. 'You are quietly content, I believe.'

'*Ecstatic*,' Lucian corrected. 'And not quietly at all. Shouting from the rooftops, in fact.'

'Where is she?' Niko glanced past him.

'Making sure everything is ready inside.' He'd not wanted her to come out in the cold.

Inside, the palace was decorated in vibrant festive ribbons and bows, while Zara stood by the enormous twinkling tree in the entrance hall—his own sparkling angel. A heavily pregnant angel.

'I wanted to come out to greet you.' Zara hurried forward to hug both Maia and Niko as they walked in. 'But Lucian bullied me into waiting in here.' She shot him a look that was both vexed and flirtatious. His favourite kind.

'I didn't want you to slip on the ice—' Lucian shrugged unashamedly and set Niko's child down.

Niko laughed. 'He's right.'

The children scampered around their feet. His firstborn, Kristyn, was round-eyed at the triplets her own age, while Niko's eldest, Kailani, took the lead. It was all chatter, giggles, full-bore chaos as all the treasure in the world tumbled about right in this room with him.

'Is there caramel apple tart?'

'Are we going to ice-skate?'

'Or ski? Can we ski?'

Protective and possessive, Lucian laughed at the endless excited requests. His daughter had made him a hostage to fortune completely, but she'd enriched his life in ways he'd never imagined possible. He couldn't wait to meet his son.

He felt Zara's arm slip around his waist from behind and turned to draw her closer still. Emotions threatened to momentarily overwhelm him—but he let them wash through. He'd got much better at allowing them, accepting them—welcoming them even. Some emotions more than others—like happiness, amusement, love. He caught Zara's eye and felt even more…bliss, anticipation. *Anticipation* of bliss.

Her hold on him tightened and she smiled. She knew he needed her close—that physical contact had become as essential and as natural to him as breathing.

Life was for living. And the life he'd built with Zara was utterly and imperfectly all.

* * * * *

If you were blown away by
Back to Claim His Crown
don't miss out on the dramatic first instalment in the Innocent Royal Runaways duet
Impossible Heir for the King*!*

Also, don't forget to dive into these other Natalie Anderson stories!

Nine Months to Claim Her
Revealing Her Nine-Month Secret
The Night the King Claimed Her
Carrying Her Boss's Christmas Baby
The Boss's Stolen Bride

Available now!

#4137 NINE MONTHS TO SAVE THEIR MARRIAGE
by Annie West

After his business-deal wife leaves, Jack is intent on getting their on-paper union back on track. He just never imagined their reunion would be *scorching*. Or that their red-hot Caribbean nights would leave Bess *pregnant*! Is this their chance to finally find happiness?

#4138 PREGNANT WITH HER ROYAL BOSS'S BABY
Three Ruthless Kings
by Jackie Ashenden

King Augustine may rule a kingdom, but loyal assistant Freddie runs his calendar. There's no task she can't handle. Except perhaps having to tell her boss she's going to need some time off...because in six months she'll be having *his* heir!

#4139 THE SPANIARD'S LAST-MINUTE WIFE
Innocent Stolen Brides
by Caitlin Crews

Sneaking into ruthless Spaniard Lionel's wedding ceremony, Geraldine arrives just in time to see him being jilted. But Lionel is still in need of a convenient wife...and innocent Geraldine suddenly finds *herself* being led to the altar!

#4140 A VIRGIN FOR THE DESERT KING
The Royal Desert Legacy
by Maisey Yates

After years spent as a political prisoner, Sheikh Riyaz has been released. Now it's Brianna's job to prepare him for his long-arranged royal wedding. But the forbidden attraction flaming between them tempts her to cast duty—and her *innocence*!—to the desert winds...

#4141 REDEEMED BY MY FORBIDDEN HOUSEKEEPER
by Heidi Rice

Recovering from a near-deadly accident, playboy Renzo retreated to his Côte d'Azur estate. Nothing breaks through his solitude. Until the arrival of his new yet strangely familiar housekeeper, Jessie, stirs dormant desires...

#4142 HIS JET-SET NIGHTS WITH THE INNOCENT
by Pippa Roscoe

When archaeologist Evelyn needs his help saving her professional reputation, Mateo reluctantly agrees. Only the billionaire hadn't bargained on a quest around the world... From Spain to Shanghai, each city holds a different adventure. Yet one thing is constant: their intoxicating attraction!

#4143 HOW THE ITALIAN CLAIMED HER
by Jennifer Hayward

To save his failing fashion house, CEO Cristiano needs the face of the brand, Jensen, to clean up her headline-hitting reputation. But while she's lying low at his Lake Como estate, he's caught between his company...and his desire for the scandalous supermodel!

#4144 AN HEIR FOR THE VENGEFUL BILLIONAIRE
by Rosie Maxwell

Memories of his passion-fueled night with Carrie consume tycoon Damon. Until he discovers the ugly past that connects them and pledges to erase every memory of her. Then she storms into his office...and announces she's carrying his child!

HARLEQUIN
PLUS

Try the best multimedia subscription service for romance readers like you!

Read, Watch and Play.

Experience the easiest way to get the romance content you crave.

Start your **FREE TRIAL** at
<u>www.harlequinplus.com/freetrial</u>.